THE BOD
Pe

As a young man, Malcolm Noble served in the Hampshire Police, a chapter of his life that provides some background to his crime fiction. He has written twelve mystery novels set in the south of England from the 1920s to the 1960s. Press reviews have emphasised his sense of place and atmosphere, his strong characterisation and first rate storytelling. Malcolm Noble lives in Market Harborough where he and his wife run a secondhand bookshop.

The Body in the Bicycle Shed is the third of his Peggy Pinch investigations.

BY THE SAME AUTHOR

Peggy Pinch Investigates
Peggy Pinch, Policeman's Wife
Murder in a Parish Chest

The Timberdick Mysteries
A Mystery of Cross Women
The Case of the Dirty Verger
Timberdick's First Case
Liking Good Jazz
Piggy Tucker's Poison
The Parish of Frayed Ends
The Clue of the Curate's Cushion
The Case of the Naughty Wife
The Poisons of Goodladies Road
Take Seven Cooks (a play)

"Parochial Policing at its Best"
(Shropshire Star)

malcolmnoble.com

The Body
in the
Bicycle Shed

Peggy Pinch Investigates

Malcolm Noble

Matador
9 Priory Business Park
Wistow Road
Kibworth Beauchamp
Leicester LE8 0RX, UK
Tel: (+44) 116 279 2299
Fax: (+44) 116 279 2277
Email: books@troubador.co.uk
Web: www.troubador.co.uk/matador

This is a work of fiction. All characters and events are imaginary
and any resemblance to actual characters and events is purely coincidental.

ISBN 978 1783065 486 (paperback)
978 1783065 769 (hardback)

British Library Cataloguing in Publication Data.
A catalogue record for this book is available from the British Library.

Typeset in 10.5pt Stempel Garamond by Troubador Publishing Ltd, Leicester, UK

Matador is an imprint of Troubador Publishing Ltd

Printed and bound in the UK by TJ International, Padstow, Cornwall

To Christine

PART ONE

CHAPTER ONE

The Day They Buried Ethel

November 1926

The retired schoolmistress linked arms with Peggy Pinch, the policeman's wife, slowing them both to a dawdle. "Put up for the chair," she whispered. (They had just buried Ethel Conlin, the founding sister of the Church Kneelers Embroidering Circle.) "I've spoken with the Willowby and Becker wives."

"They'll expect Postmistress Mary to take over."

"That's why I've spoken with them. We've the annual competition coming up against St Faith's. We'll need your gumption rather than poor Mary's wool-gathering."

"We shouldn't be talking like this," said Peggy, looking over her shoulder. "Not this afternoon. Not here." She was sure that the new vicar understood what they were discussing. He had taken up the living less than four months ago and already had a reputation for knowing more than his business. And what he didn't know, his know-it-all wife would want to find out.

The country parson stood before the church porch, his hands laid lightly across his shallow belly, his head nodding as it pivoted left and right. The smartly dressed parishioners were sombre and quiet but Reverend Nigel's new village didn't look an unhappy place. The Dowsetts and the Willowbys had withdrawn from the open grave to spend some moments at the headstones of their own departed relatives. The verger, the cellar man and Farmer Jones had wandered to the lee of the churchyard elm and were lighting their pipes. "He's good at funerals," Jones remarked. "That's three he's done and he's not given to repeating his little speeches."

Mary, the postmistress, was pretending to read the notices and handwritten messages pinned to the timber porch. "Reverend, can you have a word with Isabella?"

"Oh, dear. What has the vicar's wife been up to? Has she been upsetting?"

"No, no. It's about Michael."

But the vicar's attention was elsewhere. Moorcroft and Porter, two peas in a pod, were chattering at the crown of the church path, hoping to see something in others to gossip about.

"He says he's seen a strange woman in the village," Mary pestered. "He thinks she's someone dressed up. Well, that's what he's saying."

"Does that sounds like something my wife's at the bottom of?" Reverend Nigel doubted.

"Oh no, vicar. But she might have seen something. She spends so long at her garden wall."

"I'll speak to her, Mary."

She clutched the hem of his cassock so that he wouldn't walk away.

"I know it's probably nonsense and, you don't understand, Isabella isn't involved."

Then 'Baby' Michael, the postmistress's grown-up brother who had absented himself before the committal, returned to the graveyard with his collie bitch scampering at his heels. When Peggy saw that he meant to approach (Michael had carried a soft spot for her since their childhoods), she made a face to say that her conversation was private.

Poor Michael, he needed someone to stand with. He looked for his sister but the vicar put him off, so he veered towards the men beneath the tree, though he would find no way into their conversation.

"Moorcroft and Porter are hatching something," said the vicar. "I'm called upon to intervene, I think. Please don't worry about the dressing up, Mary. I shall talk with my wife."

4

"I am so sorry about Ethel," she said but the vicar had walked away and Mary was talking to herself. "Nobody thinks that I am but I am, truly."

She buttoned her coat collar and, muttering all the way, hurried down the path. As she passed, she heard Miss Carstairs confide, "Peggy, the books are wonky," but she didn't turn her head.

"Wonky?" breathed Peggy. "What way wonky?"

Miss Carstairs puckered her lips and moved them around, chewing on a 'tut-tut' that she didn't want to say. For how many years had she told off Peggy Pinch for clumsy alliteration and had it made any difference? "Just look at that woman. She's taken to warbling like our village duck. Lord, we can't have a woman like that in the chair. Peggy, I'm talking about significant amounts that have been received as 'goodwill' and those same amounts have been expended, two or three days later, as 'services.' Twenty five pounds on one occasion."

Goodness. That was more than Pinch brought home in a month.

The collie ran free; she wanted to show that she could trick the kissing gate. Constable Pinch had no patience for the high jinks. He thought that the dog, like her master, was a nuisance the village could do without. But Pinch was already through the kissing gate and standing on the little church green and didn't need to watch the pup leap through the swinging spars. Fingering his pipe in his pocket of his dress uniform, he watched the villagers disperse. The older ones drifted towards the vicarage where the new vicar's wife and their maid were ready with cups of tea and open sandwiches. The younger parents hurried home. There was an unspoken prohibition on children playing in the street that afternoon and too many had been left alone in the cottages during the service. Usually, the Red Lion offered ale and cobs in its back room after a burial, but not this afternoon; Ethel Conlin had spent so many years preaching against drink that it would have been wrong to use her funeral as an excuse for forgetting the licensing laws. Pinch noted that Queen O'Scots, the school-ma'am's cat, was nowhere to be seen. Odd, that. But there was nothing to draw from it. Not until later.

"The money doesn't make sense," said Peggy.

"I'll pop Ethel's books across so that you can go through them."

Not yet, thought Peggy. Today wasn't the day to explain Miss Carstairs' suspicions to her husband. "Or rather, it does make sense. A rather worrying sense."

"You mean, why record it, if you're not going to explain it?"

Peggy was thinking aloud. "Almost as if, I don't know; did she want to leave a clue?"

"Something's wrong. Peggy, put up for the chair."

The ladies resumed their quiet little steps. "I can't promise," she said. "I need Pinch's permission and I'm already in trouble."

Broken Dorothy Becker was desperate to stop sobbing. She had forced herself through the trees, believing that once she reached the familiar rutted track she could hurry to Thorruck's top field without thinking. But her limbs screamed in their sockets, her chest hurt and her belly had twisted into knots so tight that every movement, she believed, tore the tubes in her stomach and spilled blood into her lungs. She could feel it. It squeezed her little heart into shapes it had never meant to be. She wanted to run but the pain in her ribs pulled one shoulder down and made one arm useless. Her other hand reached for the ground with every yard so that she stumbled like the hideous hunchback in her storybooks.

She tried to remember wise advice from her mother, but 'put away before father gets home,' 'look after Freddie,' and 'Dorothy, leave some for your brother,' were no help.

She longed to be sensible. The two words filled her head. If God was testing her, she wanted to do well. But God had better things to do, just as her grandmother would have said, 'He can't be bothered with wicked children.' And Dorothy knew that she had become wicked.

"You'll never stand straight while you're crying," she told herself, but a mess of contradictions fed the tears. She was heading for a home that she didn't want to reach. She needed help from people that she couldn't face. And daylight, usually so good, would be worse than the night.

She thought, but wasn't sure, that she was running away from the village. So much of her world had changed. Unshakable landmarks – familiar crossed paths, the noble oak, the unjumpable ditch – were like good ideas that she couldn't string together to make reason. She needed simple rules. Like, running down hill is always good. Hurry towards noises rather than away from them. Keep going, or the night will get you.

But the pain was telling her that she had been running for too long. Her body was hurting in ways that she couldn't understand. She remembered Grandma, one Christmas morning: "Play with a broken toy and you'll make it worse, Dorothy Becker."

She dropped into a ditch and, at once, her crying was comforted away. She was only weeping now. She remembered the Grimm fairy-tale, where tiny Thumblenick had nursed a broken swallow and was rewarded by being carried off to a place where men and women did nothing evil. Dorothy understood the story so clearly now. She would stay in the ditch forever. The countryside creatures would care for her. They would show a natural sympathy for a little girl like her, because they understood things in ways that grown-ups never could. Never could, because grown-ups taught wicked lies. Lessons from Sunday school played in her head; all of them, lies. She was sure the little animals were already looking over her. Like an answer to her prayers, a draught of cold air delivered a stalk of dead bracken across the backs of her legs. "Dear father God," she began.

As the temperature dropped and the evening sky turned everything grey, Dorothy nestled deeper in the ditch, pulling twigs and debris over her. She wasn't frightened now. Every time she heard the undergrowth move, she knew that the little creatures were caring for her. Squirrels and field mice. The birds and the tiny insects. The elves and other little folk. All the world knew that Dorothy Becker had been kind to animals; now they would repay her by watching over her. She was theirs now. Just like Thumblenick and the swallows.

With no holding back, she felt herself drawn into the warm mire of gaily coloured dreams, a world of eiderdown and pillows, fairy tales and sweet treats, where the forest folk spoke as clearly as toys and dolls, wardrobes and doorknobs. So comforting that she felt and heard herself turn the key to lock herself in. Her white little fingers moved as she did it. She could hear the real world, where everything had gone wrong, but all that happened on the other side of the door. She could turn off the noises and, if the outside still got too close, she could talk herself into not seeing. She had no need to be scared because she had given herself time to sort things out, and she steeled herself to protect that.

She heard the search parties but didn't care. They were far away and would never find her. And if they did, she would never talk to them. She knew that the women would be in the church, gathered around a special heater as the messengers came in with news and went out with instructions. They would sit her mother in the vestry and feed her cups of tea, keeping her talking so that she couldn't ask questions. The gardens would have already been searched - each family looking in its own shed, then reporting to the verger in the middle of the street. The children would have been quizzed for any clues about Dorothy's favourite playgrounds. Dorothy pictured the men, with poles and nets, searching the river and water-meadows, while other patrols checked the farm buildings at Thurrocks, before progressing up the side of the valley towards the men searching from the churchyard, down. Before long, someone would suggest bringing out the lanterns and the night-time scene would be like a harvest festival with different wobbly lights showing the reach of each search party.

She felt sorry for young Grace Willowby. The others would treat the search as a grown up's game. That Becker girl would turn up, they'd be saying. 'That one's always making trouble.' But Grace would worry that Dorothy might never be found. The neighbours thought that Grace was the better one, an opinion that Dorothy had proved wrong by teasing and scaring the girl to frets. She had convinced Grace that children were stolen and cooked in ovens. Once, she had pinned her to the ground and forced her to say that Hansel and Gretel was a true story. Now, Dorothy longed to say sorry. Her bullying of her loyal, straightforward friend was all that bothered her. Every other judgement had been snatched from her.

She imagined Alice, brought before the scowling queen. 'I have nothing to say, your majesty.'

'You have nothing to say?' crowed the queen, leaning forward on the magistrate's bench, irritably tapping the gavel on the polished mahogany.

'I have nothing to say.'

'No pronouncements in your purse?'

Dorothy studied the yellow-stained eyes and the crinkled lobes of the woman's ears. 'I have nothing to say.'

The queen proclaimed, 'Be it recorded that the witness has nothing to say,' and the masons began to chisel her evidence on the walls of the court.

She wanted to ask, was it true? Had she heard that children who stayed missing until dark didn't get into trouble?

She was crying again, not, this time, because she was fleeing from something horrible but because she was hunted by those she should trust; the real world, beyond the ditch, had been turned upside down. New senses filled her head. The bruises on her back and thighs were hurting now and she knew that blood was seeping from behind her ear. She wouldn't let her fingers touch it. She didn't want to know how deep the cut was. She burned inside but that was her own fault, she said, for running too hard.

She couldn't stop her crying. The pursuers were near, calling to each other, beckoning their dogs, keeping themselves up to pace. She wanted them to be strangers - not men from her village who would wrap their arms around her, weep with her, make promises about mother and father and ask what had happened. If she wasn't allowed to stay in her fairy ditch, she wanted to go to one of the farms or a tiny room in a cottage, one or two villages away. Her prayers became a rapid fire of bargains offered up to a God she was no longer sure of. He gave no answers. Dorothy Becker would have no say. Not talking was the only control left to her.

Dorothy's cries grew shriller until, in the moments before the hound discovered her, her sobs sounded like cries for help. She felt the dog's nose against her face. Then he sat back, barked sharply three times, and the men came thrashing through the trees, not caring what they trampled on.

"Here!"

Dorothy lifted her head, hardly an inch, and saw Queen O'Scots' grey shape seated at the brow of the ditch. She had been given away by the schoolma'am's cat.

"Light a faggot!" someone was shouting. "We've got her!"

"Well done, Admiral. Well done, boy."

It seems so unfair that Dorothy Becker didn't know if she was in trouble or not.

CHAPTER TWO

The Murder

"You use soot for slugs?"

The chief constable and Pinch proceeded slowly, in step, down the garden path.

"And soot water for growth," Pinch elaborated. "Half a sack soaked in a pot."

"For how long?"

"Till it's done."

The answer was enough.

The chief constable leaned forward at the gooseberry row and took in all that he could about Pinch's method of pruning. "They're giving me no room, Pinch," he complained. "Every month, it's something new. They say I shouldn't have appointed my godson as superintendent. Good God, I said, a chief constable needs men around him that he can trust, and Brian's a good fellow. Then there's that new member from Kipps. Always putting his two penn'th in. What's a police sergeant-major, he says. Never heard of a police sergeant-major, he says. What's he do, a police sergeant-major? What's he do! I shout, 'Drill and musketry, that's what he does!' I wish you had been there, Pinch. I brought my fist down so that the table top shook. But the Kipps man hardly took time to draw breath before he's going on about the women. We need more of them, he says. Do you know, he's even called for some of the women auxiliaries to be made warranted constables? Oh, it'll come, I told him, but not in my time!"

In other circumstances, Arthur Pinch would have felt

uncomfortable, listening to these moans from on high, but a stroll in the garden seemed to be an off-duty moment. Common talk suggested that the chief constable had upset the watch committee and they wanted him out. In the old queen's time, he had been appointed by worthies who thought that his piety and high morals would do the county good, but a new generation on the watch committee found him a difficult customer who submitted his accounts to God and would answer to no one else. He summoned his superintendents for morning prayers and wrote sermons at his leisure. He spoke in difficult terms and wore brown leather calf-high boots that were difficult not to look at. Difficult grey whiskers grew up from his neck to his ears, but he shaved his cheeks, chin and lip. It gave the impression that the beard was growing up from his chest rather than down from his face. And, too often, he was caught wearing an old smoking jacket in his office.

"I mean to get out to my village stations more often. They're the heart of policing England, you know. The town bobby's grandfa' was a night-watchman but you, you're drawn from the olden stock of the parish constable." He looked Pinch straight in the face: "No one knows I'm here, you know. They think I'll be back after lunch. Well, I won't. I mean to play truant. There, what do you think of that! People don't know what's going on, Pinch. They've no idea what's behind it all. My man, bad forces are at work in our country. We need to dig them out at the roots. Poison them at their prime."

Pinch said, "I'm hoping to get some plums in, this week or next. The new vicar's making arrangements."

"Hmm. Yes, quite." He pinched his whiskers. "Er? Oh yes, I see!" He tugged more heavily at Pinch's arm. "Now, I want something from you."

"Very well, sir."

"I need your licence to buy Black Bull's Dung. Will'm, the baccy man, says that your fortnightly order takes all he can get. He won't sell me a quarter ounce."

"I'm sure there's enough for both of us. I'll put a word in when I'm next in town."

"There's something else. Tell me about the schoolma'am across the road. She could be just the woman I'm looking for."

"Our best friend," Pinch grunted, judging the chief's enquiry to be a trespass. Then, more deferentially, he said that Miss Carstairs had been the schoolmistress, for as long as anyone could remember, until five years ago. Pinch had proposed to the school board that she should be allowed to pass her retirement in the old school cottage. They even presented her with the classroom clock which now hung in her parlour.

"The classroom clock?"

"Yes, it had been bought originally at the sale of the Barton and Waters railway company. Miss Carstairs was very fond of it and used to set her own watch by it each morning."

The chief stepped back from the vegetable patch and started to walk further down the path. "I'm thinking of starting evening classes for staff and children and it seems to me that your Miss Carstairs might be the woman to get things started."

Oh, so the chief was seeking a night school leader, not feminine company.

"You've got a Scots mistress in the schoolroom now?" the chief was asking, standing over a prize specimen of a fledgling fruit tree.

"Five years, now," Pinch confirmed. "They don't see eye to eye, I'm afraid. Miss McPherson is more regimented, more of a disciplinarian perhaps, where Miss Carstairs taught each child as an individual. She knew things, you see. She was aware. She's part of the village."

The chief bent forward and sniffed. "I'd have thought you'd get no nonsense with a Scot in charge. But the Becker girl's unruly? Parents struggling to keep her on the straight and narrow?"

"Her young brother's the naughty one."

"Not surprised. I've never been surprised by the hand big sisters have in that. Were you an only child, Pinch?"

"In the middle of three, sir."

"Ah, neither fish nor fowl. I was much the same. This girl needs guidance, Pinch, away from the village, I'd say."

"We need to give her a few days. The outrage is less than a full day

13

old and the kid's hardly slept. She's not herself. She's not spoken a word to anyone but her parents have caught her telling stories to herself."

"I'm not surprised," said the chief. Every comment seemed to confirm his understanding of the case. "She knows she's done something wrong and feels too guilty to face her mother. I'll wager she agreed to meet some lad in the woods. She fancied tempting him with one or two things then found that she'd unbuttoned more than she could handle. Poor chap must be fretting." He stretched his back, put his hands in his pockets and stood back. "Grand, this is a grand garden, Pinch, a credit to the force. I always enjoy my visits. A garden brought up from hours of work, the police house immaculately kept, all business and procedures up to date. Your sergeant agrees. You're a good village blue."

"Sir."

The chief caught sight of Peggy's face at the rear bedroom window. "Ah! Your wife is back in harness."

"She can't have been far," Pinch remarked.

"Perhaps she was lying down or catching up at the front gate."

"I'll speak with her later."

"How is she, Pinch? Still something of a rebel, I hear. A mouse down some woman's back, a bucket of slops over a neighbour's head?"

"That … was some time ago."

"Only weeks ago," the chief insisted. "A month or two, perhaps. Truth is, Pinch, she's too much talked about and we can't have that. I was passing the refs room, just the other morning, and the boys were having quite a chuckle about her. The truth, Pinch. The truth is she's become a joke and if you don't step in, she'll make a joke of you. Then policing in this village will become a matter of laughs. A laughing stock, and we can't have that."

"I'll speak, sir."

"You must promise me more than that, constable. You must put your foot down with a firm hand. Draw in the reins and tighten the leash."

"Sir."

"The inspector agrees."

"Sir?"

14

"A slow and steady approach to this case. The girl's not talking and that gives you time to see what comes out of the woodwork. I'll not send a detective until you have something definite to work on."

"Sir? You said, the inspector agrees? About Mrs Pinch, sir? You've spoken? Both of you, I mean, to each other?"

"There are charities that provide sound places for girls like this Becker wretch. They'll deliver the strong hand that her parents cannot. Morals, Pinch, and they'll occupy her with hard work. Often that's enough to bring them to heel, a dose of hard work. Drill and musketry, eh?"

Pinch was worried now. Did his superior officer, talking in code, want Pinch to impose similar hard labour on his wife?

"Speak up, Pinch. What do you say?"

"Yes, sir."

"I'm on my way to talk through this case with the vicar. In a day or so, perhaps we'll meet - the vicar, the doctor and I - and decide what's to be done with the girl. Moral delinquency's the name for it. I'll be back before dark to sign the journal and registers. After that, we'll leave all village matters in your hands. What's in your shed?"

"Bicycles, sir, and some dried onions that might interest you."

"Keep it locked, do you?"

"Yes sir," Pinch fibbed, then to lessen the lie, he added, "in the night time."

The chief led the way to the little wooden shed. They heard a squad of territorials shambling away from the Red Lion. They had been detailed to clear debris from the village ford (another of the new vicar's 'arrangements').

"It must be close to one o'clock," the chief remarked and, immediately, the church clock corrected him by striking the three-quarter hour. "Have you still got that copy of Herbert's Extracts from a Country Parson?"

"I've not thrown it out," Pinch assured him. "But I can't put my hand on it. I was looking for it the other day."

"I like a good book."

"Do you want to see my dry onions?" Pinch asked, his hands on the bolt of the shed door.

15

"Your copy has an interesting inscription, if I remember."

Pinch slid the bolt free and curled his fingers around the door handle. "I'm sure you'd like to see them, sir."

But the chief was already making for the garden gate. "No, no. The book will do nicely. Have it ready for me when I come back."

So Pinch didn't open the door. He called, "I was saying, sir. It seems to have gone astray." But the chief was out of earshot and treading up the village street. "I shall enquire with Mrs Pinch," said the bobby to himself and pushed the bolt home.

That morning, Peggy had already stepped back from gossip in the post office queue, bitten her tongue at nonsense spoken at the school gates and walked by, without comment, when too many people were wanting to shop in Ruby Becker's back garden shed. So, when she heard the chief's plans for Dorothy, she was ready to steer to the sound of the guns. A wiser temper would have reminded her that it's better to let her tongue loose at old village wives than to bark at her husband. But Peggy was beyond listening to advice. She was down the stairs and into the kitchen before the chief had managed half a dozen steps up the village street.

"How dare that man suggest such a thing!" she shouted. "We won't allow him to do it, Pinch. We'll …"

Constable Pinch leaned forward, his great fists slamming on the breakfast table. "You will do nothing. You have already turned this house into a source of mockery. The men are laughing at us, Mrs Pinch. You're like some music hall turn, the butt of shady jokes. And rascally songs, I don't wonder. You heard what the chief said. Put your foot down, Pinch, he said. Put it down with a firm hand."

She knew that she was in trouble. She insisted, "He is not going to put our Dorothy into a convent," but her voice had lost its edge. Then, quietly: "She has done nothing wrong. You wait until the women of the village hear about it."

"Enough!" Pinch thundered. "Peggy, you go too far!"

Peggy said nothing and prayed that her face would say nothing either.

"The chief constable!" he bellowed. "The chief constable, Mrs

Pinch! The chief constable ..." Purple faced and choking with rage, he couldn't roar without spluttering and wiping his face. "Mrs Pinch, the chief constable goes to a police station and hears, when he goes, he hears ... He hears his men mocking us, mocking this household. Because of you!" His face, his fists, the pulse in his neck were ready to burst. "God, woman. How do I make you listen?"

Five stormy years, trauma that had left no doubt they would regret their lives together, had taught Peggy that her husband raged only when she had pained him beyond repair. Their arguments so often led to a taut, horrible silence when they both realised that they weren't talking about children, and although it took two people to engage in that, Peggy knew that it was her fault. It was her main job - wasn't it? - and each barren year that passed brought it closer to being the only duty that mattered. Usually, because they couldn't talk about it, each would avoid the other until the ghost withdrew. But this time, Pinch was so angry that silence wouldn't do.

His fists were clenched, red. His face boiled.

She knew that Pinch could never put up with being humiliated, and that's what she had done. So, she submitted. She sat at the kitchen table, laid her hands in the lap of her cheap dress and kept her face down. She felt horrible. How could she say that she had never meant to hurt him or that she would try to be a better wife than she was – words she had pleaded so often that they had lost all power? "I don't want people to laugh at you, Pinch," she said quietly. "I know it sometimes feels that I'm not trying but – they shouldn't be laughing. I've always said you're a good policeman, haven't I? And I've never said anything except you're a good husband to me."

"I've never hit you," he said.

That was the other trouble. The story that he regularly slapped her, or even took his belt to her, was so current in the village that even their best friend across the road believed it. The truth was that Pinch was so heavy handed in everything he did that he feared that, if the day came when he lost control, he'd knock her into next week.

Tears filled Peggy's eyes, "Tell me who's laughing and I'll put them right."

"You'll do no such thing!" he roared. "I don't need my wife to explain for me!" Then, in words he'd never used before, he shouted. "I'm Pinch!"

"That's not fair!" she spat, rising from the chair, though she didn't know what she meant. This whole thing was unfair, wasn't it? "Tell me what to do."

Forty seven minutes later - when Peggy was upstairs washing her face from a pitcher and bowl, when Miss Carstairs was relining her pantry shelves and the vicar was ordering tea for a vagrant on his doorstep, when Baby Michael was guiding the village duck towards a flooded ditch in the Porters' garden - Arthur Pinch found the body in his bicycle shed.

He opened the wooden door outwards and the orgy of butchered flesh and exploded blood sent him senseless. Later, Mollie Sweatman and Friar's drayman would claim that they heard him gasp before he fell but Pinch could remember only that, as he recoiled from the Ripper scene, he tripped on the shed's step. His shoulder knocked against a fence post and he fell face down with his throat on the threshold, so that his head was inside the slaughterhouse while his arms and legs were splayed in the open air. He bruised his shin as he struggled to his feet. When he backed to the garden gate, he was horrified to see that he was holding the murderer's knife. Blood still dripped from its long, rusty blade and soaked the wooden handle. Already, villagers were gathering in the lane; Pinch's face and hands, shirt and mighty forearms were covered with dead blood.

Stunned, unable to speak and wet between his legs, he sat on the grass verge while his mind collected brief, unconnected pictures of what was happening. The chief constable and the parish doctor were there. Peggy was telling the neighbours to keep clear. Silly Michael was dithering behind Peggy's back, his face curiously twisted as if he were tortured by an awkward dilemma. Up the street, the dray's steam engine choked on its own breath. Postmistress Mary, standing in the middle of the road, was waving both arms; Pinch had a peculiar notion that she was trying to stop the sheep being brought down from the top.

The village teetered on the edge of frenzy. From the moment that

Pinch disturbed the place of murder, evil had seeped out, as tangible as any poisonous mist. Women put their hands over their mouths so that they wouldn't breathe in the wickedness. The men – the roofer, the cellar man and the carter – braced themselves, ready to fight, if only they could find an adversary. The loose collie was tumbling head over heels, then rolling on her belly. Freddie Becker was crying hysterically, bounding along the hedgerows with no one to stop him.

"He didn't do it! He didn't do it!" seemed to come from the far end of the village.

"He was with me, all the time," said Peggy just loud enough for those closest to hear.

The postmistress and the Red Lion's landlady had left their businesses, the vicar's maid had been dispatched to pick up news and Jones was holding his cattle at the top of the village. Little Freddie Becker was still running up and down in tears. Several women seemed to be loosening and retying their aprons. Driver David, completing the return journey on market day three hours early, reversed his bus into the rough ground outside the school, where the Scottish teacher was barking that children were not to peer from classroom windows. Verger Meggastones' bulky figure owned the middle of the crowd. "We know you didn't do it, Pinch," he called.

Peggy stooped at his side, breaking the buckle of a shoe and pressing the knee of her skirt into the mud. She stroked his wet hair and tried to get his eyes to fix on hers. "We'll come through this, Pinch. Don't worry." She tried to take the knife from his fingers but he held tight. "Who is she, Pinch? Where's she come from?"

His face had lost all colour; his nose and eyes were swollen with unspent tears. "He's got to arrest me, Peggy." His voice seemed far away. "He has no choice. He'll take me away and lock me in the cells."

"You didn't do it, Pinch," she protested.

"Peggy, he's got no choice."

She leaned close to his ear. "Hold nothing back, Pinch. We'll say everything, just as it was. Then people will see you couldn't have done it."

"We know you didn't do it, Pinch?" a friendly voice repeated from the back.

19

The vicar hurried downhill, his white cassock billowing as he tried to gather up his flock. Some, he sent home. To the vicarage garden, he dispatched a mix of the very good and the vulnerable. "I think the older ones would welcome an open house," he said to Miss Carstairs who immediately enlisted Mrs Willowby and Mrs Porter as helpers.

"Please, no unworthy talk," he warned loudly. "No one knows the truth of what we have here." Then his face closed up as he realised that one person, at least, was burdened with that knowledge in their heart.

Peggy wanted the priest to shut up. She turned her back, hoping to shield Pinch from his attention. But he went face to face with the chief, pressing his case for the village pub to be a refuge.

The chief, who had already decided that this vicar's theology was untrustworthy, took command. "Clear the Red Lion! Take Pinch there, let him wash and drink a couple of beers. Find him a good shirt, for God's sake. But keep him there and it's out of bounds to everyone else."

The doctor was in the middle of it, his hands in his pockets, his tie loosened and showing his top button. "Twenty five minutes, I'd say. A moment or two longer, possibly, but certainly not thirty five or forty."

"Then, Pinch was in the kitchen with me all the time," Peggy said loudly. "He was telling me off in the kitchen."

The doctor spoke freely, trusting that those who needed to know would be listening. "The killer cut her throat, pulled her head back with sufficient strength to break her neck. You're looking for a beast, chief constable. He went on to stab her several times in the back. Also, a vicious gash, I'd call it a tearing, to her stomach. No one knows her, chief constable."

"She's not from round here!" someone shouted.

"Her name," said the chief constable, "is Ann Bidding."

CHAPTER THREE

An Early Arrest

Crows circled the church tower, their cawk-cawking celebrating that something wicked had been done. Edna Thurrock, alone in the fields, swore that sheep walked backwards when two o'clock tolled.

Fifteen minutes earlier, Mrs Willowby had abandoned her piano playing when the alarm went up; now the lid slammed shut in her empty cottage, its clap striking across the village sky. "Something bad," Mrs Becker and Postmistress Mary said together.

As the chief constable helped Pinch to his feet, Peggy gave in to a ridiculous impulse. She ran to close her back door, pushing the pantry window shut as she hurried along the path. It was only a moment's absence but the main players were departing before she got back to the street. Miss Carstairs and Ruby Becker were already welcoming tearful, worried ladies into Old School Cottage. She caught sight of Pinch's broad back as he turned into the Red Lion yard, and the chief was arranging a parking lot for the detectives' cars. "They're already on their way. A pair, and they won't be gone while it's light." she heard him say. The vicar was nowhere to be seen.

Those villagers who were comfortable to come more slowly to judgement stayed in the middle of the country road, noting odd details that, while not evidence of murder, weren't readily explained. A deep cycle track in the muddy verge. The victim had no handbag and no coat, as far as they could see. And the absence of the school-ma'am's cat.

"Unusual," remarked Mr Willowby.

"Not usual at all," said his wife.

That it was something bad was left unsaid.

The diehards stood shoulder to shoulder, arms crossed, feet square and not shuffling: they looked at the open shed door and waited. With the grey evening sky came the risk of rain but the villagers knew that nothing natural could wash away their evil.

"Freddie Becker?" Peggy enquired, but no one responded.

Gradually, the last of the crowd melted away. Some people went home, promising to come out again. Some spoke of old folk who shouldn't be left alone. Others looked around for the vicar who had wandered off too early. Farmer Jones brought his faithful horse and cart to the top of the street, expecting an early summons to pick up the body.

Realising that the dead body would be left unguarded if she walked off, Peggy stepped to the middle of the street and raised a hand. The horse came to attention and, on Jones' say-so, delivered the cart to the front of the police house. "We're ready to take possession of the body," he said. "Ready, when commissioned to do so."

"I really don't know, Mr Jones."

"We ought to be covering her before the drizzle, Mrs Pinch," he observed without taking his pipe from his cracked amber teeth. "Looks like drizzle, you know."

"I must find young Freddie," she persisted.

The rough old farmer pinched the pipe stem and drew it a half inch from his mouth. "You'll do well looking in the church, miss. Now, don't you go telling that I told."

Queen O'Scots observed from the leaning chimney of Bulpit Cottage. She saw the Scottish teacher, whom no one liked, in other people's gardens, and the policeman's wife walking outdoors without a hat. She heard the cellar man bolt the heavy iron brace across the Red Lion's front door, something usually done at night-time. Sensing rain, Queenie settled closer to the chimney; nothing was to be done about these out of place images. An uneasy quiet folded over the village.

The neighbourhood tramp, who had embedded himself in the corner of the graveyard, heaped layer upon layer of clothes and rags on his back and commenced his slow progress along Wretched Lane. He was beyond the village boundary before Peggy reached the kissing gate. He knew that he would be drawn into people's suspicions if he stayed.

Peggy was sure that no one had noticed young Freddie's flight, but when she got to the church, she found the vicar standing in the empty nave. For all the flowers and polished floors, it looked a cold and empty place.

"He has taken himself prisoner behind the staircase door."

Peggy was oddly conscious that she was in church with her head uncovered. She felt like an awkward schoolgirl, trying to make nothing of her error as she stood before her headmaster but knowing that he had noticed. It was a matter to come back to.

"You're good with the Becker children, Mrs Pinch. I think you should try." The vicar started to tidy the row of hymn books at the back of the pews, ready to waylay further visitors.

Peggy moved to the oak door that separated the church tower from the rest of the building. She had no motherly voice, so she spoke as she would to a friend.

"What's happened won't go away because you're hiding, Freddie."

"She saw her, Mrs Pinch, and now she's had her innards stretched and I saw her too. She'll stretch my innards just as she did to the dead 'un."

Peggy looked over her shoulder, trying to calculate how much the vicar could hear. Most of it, she guessed. "Who else did you see in the woods, Freddie?"

"I didn't see her kill that lady, Miss Pinch." The Becker children rarely managed to put Miss and Mrs in the right places.

"But she saw you playing in the woods with Dorothy, didn't she? Who, Freddie? Who saw you in the woods?"

"Miss McPherson showed me, miss. Our teacher. You believe me, don't you?"

"You're quite safe, Freddie. You know that, don't you? Now come on, let me in."

"She did things to me, miss. I only meant to show our Dorothy. I didn't know what ..." The rest was lost in his tears.

Peggy gave him time before she said, very quietly, "I know you

23

are telling one truth, Freddie, but sometimes we tell one truth so that it's easier and push another to one side. Remember what we were saying; you, Dorothy and I?"

"Half a truth is half a fib, miss."

"That's right. So we mustn't pretend and I won't pretend, dear. What you did with Dorothy was wrong but you're only a lad."

"Dorothy says girls are wicked because they're wicked; boys are wicked because they're boys." He spoke with the voice of a child wanting to make friends.

"You're not wicked, Freddie."

"I'm only a lad," he played back.

"That's right, and Miss McPherson is a grown-up so you were right to trust her, whatever she did."

"I'm only a lad."

"Freddie, did Miss McPherson see you in the woods with Dorothy?"

"No, miss. That was the lady what killed the dead 'un. 'Leave no witnesses to put him to death.' That's what she said to me before I run off. Don't you see, miss? That's why she killed the other one, and now she'll do me an' all."

Puzzled, Peggy looked to the vicar who smiled and shook his head to show that the lad had misquoted.

She persevered. "No one's going to do you, Freddie. But half a truth is half a fib. We agreed that, didn't we?"

"Some things are better not told, mother says."

"That's why Dorothy hasn't spoken to anyone, isn't it? But can you let her carry on like that? Did God mean it to be her burden? Shouldn't you speak up for her?"

"Things are a mess, miss."

She looked over her shoulder and the vicar nodded to encourage her.

"Are you sitting on the bottom step, Freddie?"

"Second one up."

"The vicar has brought me a stool."

"The one from the porch?" His voice had his mother's soft country tone; there was little of his father in Freddie Becker.

24

"I've drawn it right up to the door. I'm too big for it really. Now, Freddie, I want to be sure. You and Dorothy went into the woods where you showed her what Miss McPherson had done to you. Miss McPherson wasn't there, but another lady saw you and told you not to leave witnesses."

"That's right, Mrs Pinch," he snivelled

"The body in my bicycle shed? Was she in the woods?"

"I didn't see her but it makes sense, doesn't it? Leave no witnesses, you see."

"And the lady who spoke about witnesses? Did she hurt Dorothy?"

"Didn't see that either, because I run off. Miss, these are such bad things."

Peggy looked again to the vicar. Yes, he had noted the facts of the child's story. "For both of us, Fred," she continued, having paused for only a moment. "You were in our garden this afternoon, weren't you? I heard someone scampering about."

"I didn't see the murderer come, miss. She must have already done it."

"But you did look through our kitchen window?"

She pictured the boy wiping his nose on the back of his hand and blinking away his tears. "I won't tell, ever."

"Oh gosh, that would be terrible, wouldn't it, Freddie? People would be giggling behind my back, then saying things just loud enough for me to hear. I wouldn't be able to walk down the village street without worrying that everyone was looking at me. Yes, terrible. But I might have to tell people the truth, and go through all those awful things, if it is the only way of showing that Mr Pinch didn't kill the lady in the bicycle shed."

"I won't tell on you, miss. Not ever."

"Dorothy has got the same problem, hasn't she? If she tells what really happened in the woods, the consequences would be too awful to live through."

"What would happen if she did? Did tell the truth, I mean."

Peggy, desperately, wanted to respond to the boy's courage. "I don't know, Freddie. I suppose, it would depend on how many

25

people we had to tell. We like to keep things to ourselves in our village, don't we?" She wanted to reach through the oak barrier and take his little hand. "I can't make any promises, dear. But you can't stay shut on the stairs for ever, can you? And we can't leave Dorothy locked up either, can we?"

The vicar was at her side now. He laid a hand on her shoulder. "Freddie, who was the lady?"

"No, miss. She wasn't one of us. I'd never seen her before. Heavens, miss, it seemed only a little naughty when we was doing it, and now all this has happened. It shouldn't be, miss."

"This is going to be difficult, Freddie," she said. "Probably, it's the first grown-up thing God's called you to do. But can you shy away from it? The detectives are coming. I want you to tell them everything, and you'll have to do it while mother is with you."

Before the boy could agree, there was a clatter in the unattended porch. The great door opened and Miss McPherson stumbled into the church. She always looked scrawny and not finished off, as if she woke early in the mornings but found too much to do before leaving for work. And her shoes were too big for her feet. Verger Meggastones came two paces behind, his face red from running. Moments later, other faces filled the doorway. Ernest Becker barged through the little crowd, eager to lay hands on anyone who had molested his daughter. Meggastones and the cellar man grabbed his shoulders. Jasmine Moorcroft shouted, "We'll get her for you, Becks!" but took no step forward.

The old building seemed to shudder with dry ehoes. Freezing chills swept along the aisles.

"Everyone!" the vicar called out. "This is God's house."

A scurry of stalks and leaves spiralled in a corner of scrubbed uneven slabs, as if the sorcerer's apprentice was in the place. Tricks of light brought angry colours to the tall windows of stained glass. Frighteningly tall, at that moment.

The woman was ready to fall to her knees. "I must talk to him."

"We can't allow that, Janet."

"I want to tell him everything's all right," she pleaded, her accent thickened by her distress.

"The verger will take you to his cottage. As far as we know, Mr Meggastones, Janet McPherson has done nothing wrong. Everyone, I want you away from the church path."

Now that the Red Lion was clear, except for Pinch in the window nook and the landlady who was finding things to do at the counter, Queen O'Scots traipsed through from the kitchen and stretched herself before the hearth of the winter log fire. The vicar had invited housewives for tea. Those who were shy of going to the big house at the top of the village, or had yet to take to the new vicar's wife, were assembling in the old school-ma'am's cottage. Ladies' feet would be everywhere; Queenie needed an alternative sanctuary. A warm room with Pinch seemed a good place to be. He was unlikely to be bothered by others. The cat could sense a gruesome death as much as anyone in the village but, though something was wrong here, Pinch had no wicked aura about him.

He made his pint last twenty minutes and when he'd finished, the landlady brought a second, free of charge. The chief couldn't get in because she had put the bolts on – he tried the front and back but, though he shouted through the letterbox, he couldn't make her hear. He rapped on Pinch's window, then stood on the flowerbed so that they could talk across the open windowsill.

"I've made some decisions," he said.

When the chief decided to do things without the guidance of others, the police force held its breath.

Pinch leaned out of the window and said quietly, "Chief, I can't afford to be suspended."

"Lord, I'm not sending you off duty. Pinch, I didn't get to speak with your new vicar. He wasn't about. So I came back to the police house. Something was going on between you and Mrs Pinch, that was clear. Quite a row and I didn't want to interrupt by knocking on your door."

"Oh," said Pinch, gripping the window frame. "I see, sir. I was putting my foot down with a firm hand."

"Pinch, you didn't kill Ann Bidding; you were plainly busy at the time." Then the old man winced and reached down to pull his trousers free of his crotch. "Grief, man, I've been stung. Damned nettle up m'inside leg. Damned jungle of a flowerbed, this is."

Pinch eased back from the window. "I'll get her to unlock."

"No, no, man. Boots are filthy. Better we talk through the hole in the wall."

An upstairs window clattered open.

"Grief!" yelled the chief as scalding water tipped from a boiling pan, most of it missing him by a couple of paces but some splashing his muddy trousers.

"I'll bring you a beer, chief," said Pinch and he stepped towards the counter.

"Fine, man. I'm perfectly fine."

When Pinch returned to the windowsill with two pints of beer, the chief constable was wafting spiders' threads from his face and smelling his fingertips for something suspicious. Pinch was sure that the chief wanted to blow his nose and went as far as offering a handkerchief.

"Ah, yes. Got my own. Well spotted, man." He made a big show of clearing his tubes, sunk half the pint in one go, then asked, "What do you make of your verger, Pinch? I met him at the vicarage gate. Young Michael had told him that the postmistress couldn't be found. Meggastones was going to look for her in the vicarage. What's that all about?"

"But she was in her post office. We all saw her come running out."

"So what was the verger up to?"

"I can't say, sir. Except, he's a good man."

"What do we know about this Ann Bidding?"

"Chief, I have never seen her before." Pinch's voice croaked with desperation. "She's a stranger to this village, that's all I can say."

"I got a letter from her, two weeks ago, pleading for her brother who had been unfairly sacked. His employer suspected him of theft but, according to Miss Bidding, no one in his family believes he's a thief. I passed it to Fisher but promised nothing."

"Who did the brother work for?"

"Saunders and Lakey."

"Ah, the solicitors who employ the Becker father. I'll have a word with him."

"No, Pinch. We can't have you policing up and down this street. It wouldn't be fair on you or the village. I'm sending you to help on Constable Brevitt's beat until this matter is settled. He's on the edge of retirement, you know. Too much of a crock to do anything useful. Don't worry, there'll be plenty of policemen here, come tomorrow."

"You're moving me, sir?"

"Attaching you, Pinch. A temporary measure, no more than that." The chief wrapped fingers around his chin as he considered another point. "Of course, that does leave your wife here, unsupervised."

A parent's shout from across the street turned the chief's head.

"Away from that window, Grace Willowby, and back in your bed!"

"What's going on?" the chief asked quietly. "Here, Pinch, what do you make of it?"

PC Pinch stood on his toes, hitched his belt on the window-frame and leaned forward, pressing his weight on the chief's shoulder as his top half protruded from the pub's window.

"There's nothing to see!" shouted the mother again.

Two detectives were leading Miss McPherson across the church green, towards two police cars at the gate.

"An early arrest?" Pinch wondered.

A third detective was approaching at the double, saluting his superior with an exaggerated semaphore wave of his arm. "She asked to be taken into custody."

"Young Fisher," sighed the chief before the officer was in earshot. "Common pedigree and two inches too small. But good at some things." Then, more loudly: "Is this an arrest, Fisher-boy?"

"Evidence from a child, I'm afraid, chief. But others may come forward. Probably ..."

"Probably too many wrong ends from a bunch of sticks, Fisher. You can't listen to unhappy children. You need something to put before a court, boy."

"It's the schoolteacher, chief. She asked us to take her in. Fair, all round, she said. Better that she wasn't left here in the village until the truth is sorted." Then, because the chief might not have known: "Miss McPherson is Scots, sir."

"Asked?" he spluttered through his ale. "Asked, did she? My police headquarters is not a blessed hostel, young Fisher."

The chief wiped his forehead and said, as the detective disappeared into the Beckers' home and the police car drove through the village with the schoolteacher on board, "I want you out of the way before supper, Pinch. We're not coping, not coping well at all. Every step we take forward, we'll have to step back from later."

The vicar was the first to tell Peggy that her husband had moved. He and Peggy were walking down from the church. "I understand. The police house is your home and you'll want to stay there, but you are always welcome at the vicarage. We have a very private bedroom in the annex. Isabelle is very fond of you. The village is going to need you, Mrs Pinch. Need you, to work very hard."

Peggy said nothing. The village had quietened down. Her neighbours were settled in their parlours. Pinch had gone and the Red Lion was ready to open for the evening.

"How did you know that Freddie had interfered with the poor girl?" the vicar asked.

"She has a name, vicar."

"Quite so."

"It was clear from the start," Peggy explained. "Freddie was the only person that Dorothy would keep quiet for."

"How very shrewd."

"But, vicar, we must always listen carefully to children. Freddie said that he ran off before the woman attacked Dorothy, meaning …"

"… meaning," continued the vicar, "that the boy's experimenting was not the most serious assault on the girl. The lad has no doubt that it happened. I fear for him. I fear, if he heard something dreadful but could do nothing about it."

They stood in the middle of the lane, halfway between Miss Carstairs' Old School Cottage and Peggy's police house, and stared at where the body had been; the shed door was still open. "The passage is from Deuteronomy," he said. "Chapter 1, verse 7. The hands of the witnesses shall be the first upon him to put him to death. Of course, Freddie may have misheard it but I don't think so. Who is it, Mrs Pinch, evil enough to come into our parish and corrupt the scripture to justify murder?"

"Let's hope she's an outsider, vicar." Queen O'Scots stepped between them and, across the road, the mother duck without her brood sunk into the shadows. "Your text for Sunday?"

"Oh, that will come in the quiet hours," he said, walking her to her gate. "I fancy I'll step into Belle's sittingroom when she's at her needlework. Peculiar, how she'll cock her head in a certain way or twist her fingers."

"She's your inspiration?"

"I'm not a vicar who sits in his study, Mrs Pinch. Yes, in a peculiar way, I think you're right."

Peggy wondered if the vicar's wife had awkward shoulders. The evening breeze chilled her ankles. She was ready to go indoors. "Good night, vicar."

At half past nine that night, Peggy drew the table lamp closer so that its yellow light shone down on the account book of the Church Kneelers Embroidering Circle. As she worked through the columns of figures, she sensed Ethel's neat voice. The solution would seem so easy when it came but, at the beginning, Peggy had no idea what she was looking for. She ferretted through the pages and got nowhere for an hour. She couldn't get rid of the idea that the answer would be found in the schoolbooks, not these accounts of the sewing circle, but that was because of something she had suspected for weeks. Probably, nothing to do with Ethel's adding up. The rest of the police house was dark and eerily quiet. No one passed down the lane, even the church chimes were muted by low clouds. Queen O'Scots had crept into the house, uninvited; the cat stretched herself on the hearth rug but didn't feel at home, so she nestled at Peggy's crossed ankles beneath the writing table.

The circle had received the mystery donations on four occasions and, between three and ten days later, had settled matching payments for services. But the intervals weren't exactly the same and the donations, at first, didn't seem timed at any special occasion.

"I can't see it," she sighed, closing the ledger and pushing herself back from the table. She walked through her kitchen and, collecting a Black Cat cigarette and a box of matches from the drawer, she went to her back door step. So often this had been her 'thinking step' but tonight she tried to keep her mind clear. If she thought of nothing, perhaps something would occur to her. Queen O'Scots ventured outside. The cat listened for any sounds of supper in Pinch's vegetable patch, then retreated to the bicycle shed, then wandered off into the night.

Peggy knew that Ethel had used the accounts to provide clues that something wrong was happening. Something wicked perhaps, and Peggy felt not only frustrated that she couldn't interpret the evidence but deeply responsible for letting Ethel down. She went back to work.

Ethel had been so determined to point enquiries in the right direction that she had even marked any festival Sundays before and after the donations. This proved to be the key. Peggy leaned closer to the writing, the pad of her forefingers stroking the handwriting. The festival dates had been written in paler ink. Ethel had watered it down, probably because she was running out and wanted it to last longer. So, she must have added these annotations at a later date but together on the same occasion. What was she trying to say?

Peggy found an old envelop and, on the back, wrote down the dates of the donations, the settlement of the fees and, in two instances, the festival of the preceding Sunday. With only half an idea, she went to the police desk in the lobby, checked a date and the bishop's signature in the police house journal (the 24R, as it was known), then slapped the book shut.

"Got it."

"Got it," she repeated as she pushed her feet into boots, wrapped a coat around her shoulders and collected both journals. "Don't say that I haven't."

She hurried across the unlit lane and knocked urgently at Old School Cottage. The bedroom window opened and Miss Carstairs, who went to bed in a headscarf during winter months, leaned out.

"It's bishops, Bidding and books!" Peggy called up.

Without a word, Miss Carstairs closed the window, making sure that the noise of the latch emphasised her irritation. "Clumsy alliteration is neither smart nor clever," she grumbled as she descended the dark staircase. Queen O'Scots got between her feet and she had to pause halfway or fall down the rest. "What are you doing indoors?" She shook her head. "How many times have I told that girl?"

She opened the door. "You'd better come in."

The retired school-ma'am lodged a new log in the grate to rekindle the fire and directed Peggy to make herself comfortable at the hearth while she prepared a tea tray in the kitchen. Peggy settled herself in an armchair and went through her books again to make sure that she had the dates and figures to hand. The old school clock, the retirement present from the board, tick-tocked loudly on the wall behind her.

Miss Carstairs called through as she assembled the cups and teapot: "You should use it only to emphasise your point. As you come to the end of your argument, instead of repeating words you have already employed, you bring forward alliteration to convince your listeners with a flourish. You cannot alliterate in everyday talk, or simply because the words are handy, without reducing the phrase to a nursery rhyme. Peggy, I have told you, more than once."

"I'm sorry, Miss Carstairs."

The old lady placed the tray between them, pushed her back heavily into her own, very comfortable, chair and said, "Now, what have you got to tell me?" Peggy noticed that she had wrapped extra socks around her ankles.

"On three occasions, we received donations and, within two weeks, paid out similar amounts in consideration of unspecified services. Each occurrence coincides with the theft of a book. On the first occasion, the gift was preceded by the bishop's visit to our church. I don't know if any books subsequently went missing."

"You said it did on every occasion."

"Not on that occasion, I can't. On the second occasion, the

donation followed the bishop's visit to the school board. I remember the date ..."

"As I do," remarked Miss Carstairs. "It was my suggestion that he should be invited to observe our proceedings."

"I am sure that Janet McPherson mentioned that Bredon's Records of our Parish went missing a few days later, but I can't be sure."

"In my day, I would have logged such a loss in a breakages register. I don't know if she has discarded the system. She has altered so much. We can check."

"Is she back yet?"

Miss Carstairs shook her head. "So unfair if they lock her up for the night."

"Usually, the sergeants will place a lady on her honour to lodge at The Star. I can't believe they would lock Janet McPherson in the cells."

Miss Carstairs preferred to stir tea rather than comment on her successor's sense of honour. She passed a saucer of water biscuits. "Have you noticed that Queenie is looking after our mother duck? Curious, almost as if she knows that something is wrong with the brood which we don't."

"The third occasion is an exception," she said cautiously; her old schoolma'am had shown no interest in moving on to the next stage. "There was no preceding visit by the bishop, but Ethel recorded donation number three, reflected by a payment later in the week. In the meantime, Ann Bidding's bother had been dismissed from his office after the theft of a book, Ernest Becker says."

"But Peggy, really, you can't ..."

"Ann wrote to the chief constable, without satisfaction, so she followed him, here, to our village. You see, she wasn't here to meet Pinch. She came to talk face-to-face with the chief constable. Perhaps, to tell him what she knew."

"Peggy, I won't let you carry on."

"There is another occasion. Occasion number four, although it occurred some weeks before Bidding's dismissal. I'm counting it although Ethel wrote no record of it in her accounts. It followed another of the bishop's visits to our village. He called at the police house and Pinch insisted that he signed our day book. That evening, Pinch noticed that Herbert's Extracts from a Country Parson was missing from the bookcase. Don't you see?"

Miss Carstairs dipped her head to indicate her wariness. "You mean he didn't need to channel any funds through our accounts, because he had taken the book himself rather than engaging an agent? Peggy, this is very serious, what you are saying."

"Now, I need to prove it."

CHAPTER FOUR

"We Must Go Alone"

Because Arthur Pinch was lodging with the vicar of St Faith's, Peggy needed no excuse to get up a four-thirty the next morning. She collected her bicycle from beneath the kitchen window and wheeled it through the back gate, thinking that she was less likely to be seen that way. But the village was never fast asleep. The cellar man, waiting for Poacher Baines to deliver some game for the Red Lion, withdrew to the shadows as Peggy pedalled down the footpath towards the village ford. Mollie Sweatman was smoking at an upstairs window and wondered what the policeman's wife was up to. Two children, awake in their beds, heard Peggy brake and wobble as she crossed the shallow water and turned into a narrow lane, hidden between tall hedges.

Being out of doors early contributed to the holiday feeling of a day that wouldn't be governed by Pinch's comings and goings. She planned nothing out of the ordinary; twenty minutes in the post office, a cuppa with Alice in the back of the Red Lion and the meeting of the Church Kneelers Embroidering Circle before a cold lunch. That afternoon, she would dust and polish from top to bottom so that Pinch could be proud when he returned. Stubbornly, he wouldn't mention it but that didn't matter. Instead, he would go straight to the lost property book, the key register, the cash book and the post ins-and-outs - books that Peggy had taken over even before they were married. (Exquisite handwriting was a skill that Miss Carstairs had drilled into her.) She would make sure these ledgers were up to date. She would try to find a couple of entries that she could make in the day journal, so that he could see she had kept the business running during his absence. Thank God, she wouldn't have to lay his clothes out; Pinch's underpants were things she would never take to. He wouldn't want her to touch his razors, set in order by the downstairs washstand. But she would make sure that his best and second-best pipes were on show; he would be missing them already. Her holiday feeling had nothing to do with avoiding chores; it was just a day off from accounting to Pinch for every minute and timing herself for his convenience. And how lovely that she wouldn't need to waste those forty minutes – doing nothing and keeping quiet – while he napped after his lunch.

She had to wait in the lane for only a few minutes before Mr Becker came rattling along, his pedal knocking against the metal chain guard. With his knees and elbows sticking out, his head prone forward over the handlebars, and a cloth bag secured over the front wheel and his brief case buckled to his crossbar, he looked like a caricature of the village clown. He approached the ford at speed and managed it so expertly that Peggy had hardly pushed forward when he clattered past the junction. She steered in a wide circle but still had ground to make up.

"I can't go slowly for you, Mrs Pinch," he shouted. "I've got to be at work before seven and I like to be early. Six thirty if I can."

"I want to talk about the children," she called.

"I've got to make the crossroads before the smoke of the five-twenty billows over the trees of Arden Wood. Otherwise, I won't pass Jonesy's before the lad drives his flock onto the road. Then, I'll have no chance. I've got to push on."

"Of course, Mr Becker. Of course." She decided to waste no more breath on persuasion but to concentrate on catching him up.

Men, she decided, (or other people's grandmothers) liked to design women's clothes that would never be suitable for cycling. Managing her skirt took more effort than pedalling and steering and, all the time, she had to keep her coat tail from getting caught in the chain or the back wheel. She needed to lean forward to get the best purchase on the pedals but backwards to keep the saddle in place. Because the steering was loose, she felt a need to attempt to squeeze the two ends of the handlebar together, which did no good at all. But, by bringing all her strength to push down with her thighs, she slowly narrowed her distance from the bicycle ahead.

"A mother and father know when children are telling the truth," Becker was shouting. "Ruby and I have got to stand up for them but, at the same time, fight off this ridiculous talk of Dorothy being incarcerated and Freddie consigned to a school of monks."

"Don't worry. I'll look after them."

"God woman! Their mother and father can look after them!" He shouted, "I'll kill the man who ruined my Dorothy. I'll shoot him before you or anyone else gets to him!"

Before the crest of the hill, Peggy had fallen too far behind to call out, but downhill gave her the advantage. Mr Becker needed to brake softly or risk losing his cloth bag while Peggy cast caution aside, stuck her legs forward and her shoulders back and let freewheeling do the rest.

"The dead woman's brother!" she shouted as she drew level.

"Nothing can be done for him. Joe Bidding, you mean. The bishop pleaded his case in front of the younger Lakey but the firm won't be moved. Stealing's stealing and they won't put up with it. Watch out, Mrs Pinch!"

Peggy had turned her head to hear as she rattled ahead of him and didn't see the farmer's lad open the five bar gate at the bottom of the hill. The first of the sheep were already in the road when she braked, wobbled and stopped herself by steering into the grass verge. She didn't fall off but her front wheel wasn't pointing where her handlebar said it should be.

"I can't, Mrs Pinch!" shouted Becker, accelerating as hard as he could. "I can't be caught in the sheep."

Sheep were everywhere, more sheep than the lad could shepherd and, because he had no dog to marshal them, they took over the carriageway and the verges. Half a dozen were running in both directions on the other side of the hedge. Some tried to jump. Others got caught as they tried to push their way through the greenery.

Neither the sheep nor the boy turned their heads as they left her dishevelled on the grass bank. She dusted herself down, then took off her gloves and picked debris from her hair. Her hat had been tipped sideways and all of her hairpins had gone. She had a silly idea that fleas might have laid eggs on her scalp which would hatch and eat into her head. A childish worry. She recalled her mother saying, "Mites' eggs! You don't know where they come from or what they get up to!"

And that thought prompted an idea for new mischief. Of course, it was no more than the vaguest fancy to start with but who could tell how it would grow? "You'll do no such thing, Peggy Pinch," she told herself.

At that moment, awake in her bed, Dorothy Becker wanted to gouge her insides with a fork. She wanted to soak her bed with her own blood and keep digging until she brought her giblets out. When she closed her eyes, she could feel the fork probing inside her. When she slept, she dreamt that when she opened her eyes she would see the fork dangling before her, still dripping with her blood. She thought she remembered talking to the itinerant butcher about the different bones and flesh in a body, though really she had never spoken to the man. Like her conversations with Grandma, the voices were hard and palpable. When she woke, she went to the stairhead and heard mother and Freddie clattering cutlery on their breakfast dishes, and she was sure she would end up doing it with a knife.

"We've heard quite enough."

Miss Carstairs was talking to herself. She stood at the bottom of her staircase and straightened her hat and scarf in the mirror. Cock-a-leekie was cooking slowly in the kitchen, her knitting was on an arm in the parlour ready to be picked up at one o'clock and Queen O'Scots was curled at the landing window. "The woman needs to be told," said Miss Carstairs. She checked that her purse was at the top of her handbag so that she could easily pop her key inside when she had locked the front door. (The old school-ma'am had no time for ladies who dithered on their own doorsteps.) "Right-oh!" It was a quarter to ten.

Queenie was so in tune with what was going on that she was

settling herself in the hedge bottom before Miss Carstairs reached the garden gate and without the lady knowing how the cat had left the house. She glanced at the police house; there was no sign of life. Across the road, Postmistress Mary was lettering special offers on her shop window with whitewash. It was too runny because she was always too mean to do a job properly. Miss Carstairs tut-tuttered but miserliness was next to godliness, she supposed.

Nurse Cheyney held her bicycle against her tummy as she latched the Becker's front gate, then scooted to meet her.

"Miss Carstairs, has Ruby stepped beyond her gate since it happened? I mean properly, not just to her shop at the back. I think she should. I've told her that it does no good, waiting at her daughter's bedside, night and day."

"Quite right, Cheyney. We've been remiss. I'll arrange a roster and we'll take turns to sit. Has Dorothy spoken?"

"Not a word, other than mumbles to herself. It is worrying. Ruby says that she talks to her grandma, but Dorothy can't possibly remember the old lady."

"Of course not," Miss Carstairs agreed. "Dead before her time, pardon me. Now, what about the chief constable's meeting with the doctor and the vicar?"

Although Nurse Cheyney wanted to cycle downhill towards the ford, she allowed Miss Carstairs to lead her to the top of the village. "The vicar agreed to look for a charity to take the child in but, between you and me, he means to take no steps in the matter. It was a question of keeping the old police chief quiet. How are you, Clemency? What about your swelling?"

"I can manage with it. Some days, it's hardly there."

"I do wish you would tell the doctor about it. He's really very good."

"I've time enough."

"And what about Peggy?" the nurse pressed. "I've not seen her this morning."

Miss Carstairs was ready to point out that the police house curtains were open, but she decided it was none of the nurse's business.

The couple parted. Nurse Cheyney got going, hoisting herself onto the spongy saddle, while Miss Carstairs set a determined course for the vicarage garden. Then the orange box gave way beneath the postmistress's feet and she and the whitewash went down with a clatter. Mollie Sweatman and Alice, the pub cleaner, came from nowhere to help her onto her feet and, although the nurse applied her noisy back brake, the women waved her by.

"Do you want me?" called the vicar as he crossed from his house to his church.

"Later, perhaps." Miss Carstairs wouldn't be diverted. "I've got to spend a couple of minutes on the flowers, later."

"Oh dear, whatever's happened?"

The post office was too far away for the vicar to pick up the details of the accident. The women were helping Mary into her shop. Miss Carstairs hoped that he wouldn't interfere.

"I've got the ..." He flipped open his parson's pocketbook to check on appointments that he was already aware of. "Yes. Things, you see."

"Perhaps a word later, vicar. This afternoon or after tea, but you really must try not to be on the spot all the time. The village doesn't want it, vicar. We're just not used to it."

"Oh, Lord. I fear your pussy has paddled, Miss Carstairs."

The calamity had tipped the can of whitewash into the street and Queenie, unusually careless, was leaving paw prints as she patrolled towards the Pinches' house. Ruby Becker looked from Dorothy's bedroom window but no one noticed her.

Miss Carstairs expected the vicar to deliver an appropriate biblical quotation, but he failed to come up with one and was halfway up the church path when he raised an arm: "I'll be in the vestry until eleven, Miss Carstairs. We need to talk about the embroidering circle."

The vicar's wife, close to the garden gate, heard the exchange and was ready for Miss Carstairs' appearance at the dry-stone wall. She had laid a cushion at the edge of the grass so that she could kneel as she tended a flowerbed. A wicker basket for weeds was at her side, with a trowel, hand-fork and probe close by. An old pair of gloves had been discarded over her shoulder. She looked like a woman who was practised in what she was doing and knew the meaning of hard work but Miss Carstairs remained reluctant to offer too much respect.

"Stop telling stories, Belle Fripps."

Isabelle leaned back from the flowerbed and placed the trowel, neatly, in the wicker basket. "Why, Miss Carstairs. I didn't hear you coming."

You certainly did. Another fib, decided the canny old school-ma'am. "You were known as a storyteller in your husband's last living and we'll thank you not to bring your old habits to our village."

"Do come inside. Don't you think we should talk about this over a pot of tea?"

Miss Carstairs chewed her tautly puckered lips as she tried to swallow her irritation at the woman's smug confidence. The retired teacher felt that she was being quietened down, just as she used to treat angry children. Worse –much worse, she decided, as she followed the woman up the cinder path – the vicar's wife walked like a woman who had always wanted to do ballet. Deliberately, Miss Carstairs waddled. Then she decided that she wasn't waddling enough so she waddled more deliberately.

The village was proud of its vicarage garden. Although the parishioners were accustomed to truculent relationships with their parsons, a succession of ladies of the vicarage had recognised that their caretaking responsibilities went beyond handing over the half acre in a tenantable condition; they were meant to develop the gardens. Go back two hundred years and the village had been demonstrably at odds with three generations of vicars, a suspicion that was so embedded in the bones that both sides felt that each new parson was on probation until opinions were settled. If the vicars' wives had been of lesser quality, the house and gardens might have been considered too important to be left to clerical couples, but the last three had been hands on and got their fingers dirty and directed matters so precisely that gardeners and maids felt that they had been reduced to fetchers and carriers, although no professional gardener ever, truly, does as he is told. Reverend Nigel's predecessor had been a single man and an informal committee emerged to make sure that horticultural progress was not neglected. The pride went so far that each cottager accepted a duty to supply the vicarage with cuttings of their prize produce.

"You're going to be cross with me," she said as she led Miss Carstairs through the passageways of the vicarage. "I've moved all the little trinkets from the trophy room. I know that the vicars have assembled the collection over the years but I told Nigel that we needed a ladies sittingroom and the trophy room, overlooking the side lawn, seemed ideal." She opened the door. "You see, the pool with Peter Pan in the middle is just the other side of the french windows. We can open them if you like. Don't you think it was a waste to fill the room with so many fishing cups and stuffed birds?"

Miss Carstairs looked around. "The vicar rumbles in his grave," she remarked without serious rebuke. "He started the trophy room in my mother's time."

"The vicar? Oh, I can never understand this precedence. Nigel is the new vicar. Our predecessor ..."

"The old vicar."

"Yes. He had a sporting dalliance with a farmer's wife, I've heard."

"Reverend John was before him and he was incumbent for so long that no one can imagine a time before him. He is the vicar."

"Ah," mouthed the new man's wife, amused.

"Go back further and, I think, there was a doctor."

"Yes, yes. His portrait's on a wall somewhere. 1786-1872. He can't have been working all that time. The dates must be his birth and death."

"You have his books on butterflies and birds' eggs. They were supposed to be famous."

"I'm afraid, Miss Carstairs, we don't and Nigel is very cross about it. They've gone missing. They were here, I promise, when I moved, but Nigel tried to find them last week and simply couldn't put his hand on them."

"Belle Fripps, I haven't come here to discuss our history with

43

rectors. You told Edna Thurrock that Pinch couldn't have done the murder because you saw the to-do in the Pinch kitchen, seconds before they found the body."

"How do you know what I said?"

"I got it from Mollie Sweatman."

Isabelle sighed. "I made Edna promise not to tell."

"You cannot have been at the Pinch window. You were tending your garden at the time. Looking for Porter, you told Postmistress Mary."

Gosh, she was cool. "You've misunderstood. I was telling Edna what I thought had happened, how I thought things would have been, if I'd been there to see it. You got your story from Mollie Sweatman? Well, I got mine from dear Mary's brother."

"And he?"

"I think, from the new schoolteacher. But you must ask him." The lady of the vicarage was determined to make nothing of it. "Tell me, do you like the modern way; milk first?"

"Nurse Cheyney has convinced me to take my tea without milk."

"So coarse, don't you think? Putting milk in the cup before tea. It's what you see in corner houses. Office girls do it, I believe." She sighed, "How is the embroidering circle going? I know Nigel is concerned. He's so determined that we should push St Faith's into second place. "

Through the window, Miss Carstairs observed the vicar lead Gary, the Willowby son, to the gardener's shed. She couldn't believe that the boy was in trouble; the Willowbys were known to be the best behaved children in the village.

Once inside, the vicar tossed a musty apple the lad's way and searched a table drawer for one of this old redundant pipes. He found an envelope of small change that he immediately recognised. The housekeeper had asked for some extra money beyond her regular budget that morning and he had produced the amount from his pockets. Even in a countryside parish, it was difficult to keep the vicarage table stocked with good food. No doubt the money had

44

been left for some tooth-fairy or other to spirit away in exchange for a treasure that would appear, cooked and well-dressed, for supper in days to come.

"Now then," he said, trying to settle himself against a bundle of hoes and rakes. "Let's be clear. Whatever is said must be shared with your mother."

The boy hesitated. "If you think that's best, your reverence. After you've heard it all, you might be able to talk to people. I thought, quietly."

The vicar wasn't sure about that. The Willowbys were not only the best behaved but also the best tell-tales in the village. Nevertheless, preliminaries settled, the testimony came in a rush.

"It's not fair. Mistress Mary in the post office gave the paper round to Ginger Whittle." A girl. "But she said I could do tea-times, with the evening papers and the late Gazette on Fridays. Then she found out that I was running other errands at the same time and now she says I'm not fit for either round, mornings or evenings."

"Hmm," said the vicar. The old pipe wasn't suited to his new brand of tobacco.

"That's not fair."

"Well, it does seem that there might be a solution to please all around, but what about deceit, Master Willowby. After all, your pocket money from Mistress Mary was for delivering newspapers to her customers, not for further enterprise."

The boy pressed his case. "So you will speak?"

The vicar dipped his head and looked through his long grey eyebrows. "Deceitfulness is not a lapse we can let go, unnoticed."

"What do you think, sir?"

"I think I found a jumble of old ironmongery behind the old vestry door. You might sort out what's to be thrown away while placing at our kitchen door anything that might be useful. Of course, if you clean any such brass or painted metal, the task could take you longer than repentance requires."

"I don't mind that, sir, if ..."

"No bargains, Master Willowby, and I expect your mother to tell me all about it in a day or two."

That, thought the boy, was the hardest part. He polished the apple on his trouser pocket and dithered on his feet.

The child watched as the vicar came to a decision. The huge hands braced the edge of the table; as the powerful figure rose from his chair, poor Willowby seemed to shrink within himself. "Young man, we have yet to deal fully with this matter. Follow me."

Little Gary had heard stories of horrible punishment being metered out in the vicarage. He had suffered several smacked legs in his young life – show him a child who hadn't – but he had never been properly beaten. As he followed the vicar along the path to the house, he reflected on the minor steps that had landed him in this trouble. His jealousy of Ginger Whittle. His decision to make up for the lost opportunity of extra pocket money by accepting extra errands in the postmistress's time and then preferring to keep it secret from her. He never thought that his enterprise would lead to this. He composed a prayer in his head; he even made four lines rhyme but the neatness of the stanza made no difference to the vicar's determined stride.

Postmistress Mary, standing on the brow of the churchyard, saw him being led through the back door to the scullery. The boy was overwhelmed by an awesome dread that turned his stomach, chilled every bone and made every heartbeat pound in his ears.

The women were still talking in the sittingroom. A push and pull carpet sweeper was being worked on the landing. The senior housekeeper was talking to herself, complaining, in the walk-in larder. Thank goodness, none of them saw Gary being taken into the vicar's study.

He had been told that there was no shame in crying under a beating; everyone did. But he was expected to hold back the tears for as long as he could. The boy was biting his lip and digging his fingernails into other fingertips. He was sure that he wouldn't pass muster. He tried to listen to what the vicar was saying but he couldn't concentrate through his fear. He picked up little details of the room. The faded pattern on the carpet, the lines of crammed bookshelves, the rich smell of polished old furniture. Gary Willowby had never been in such a posh and well-stocked place. He wanted to say, 'I've

46

already learned my lesson, sir,' but this wasn't a room where children spoke uninvited.

"In regular circumstances," said Reverend Nigel as he opened a glass-fronted cabinet, "you wouldn't be given one of these until your confirmation, but I think the gift is timely. Here -" He handed the child a thin, pocket-sized volume wrapped in fawn covered card. Through the tears in his eyes, Gary read, 'My Prayer Book for Men and Boys, Introduced by Two Archbishops.' "Take it away, young man, and read it closely. Straightaway, tell your mother what you have done and show your vicar's present. It may help you escape further punishment. Now, off you go."

Little Gary turned, walked to the heavy door and turned again. He nearly said, 'If you need me to help with other chores ...' but he thought better of it.

"You're a good boy," the vicar said, and the young Willowby was left to find his own way out of the big house.

When, as they walked together towards the church, Peggy Pinch learned that the expensive book had been missing from the vicarage since the third week in May. She nodded with satisfaction. "A little more mystery, a little more understanding," she said softly.

The eleven o'clock meeting of the Church Kneelers Embroidery Circle was relieved to receive the vicar's wife's apologies. (Isabelle Fripps wasn't one to natter in the way of needlewomen and some older maids had yet to take to her.) Upright wooden chairs were brought to a circle and the regulars got quickly to business. As the thimbles and needles worked away, Postmistress Mary was elected to the chair and Miss Carstairs offered to be secretary. She asked that the duties of a treasurer should be kept separate, and everyone was happy to consider Peggy for that role; it would keep her mind off things, they thought. But before the matter was settled, a buzz of traded winks and nods told Miss Carstairs that neither Mrs Willowby nor Mrs Becker had kept quiet about her ambition to take charge of the circle. The postmistress reminded the meeting how hard Mrs Porter had worked for the parish in recent weeks and what about Mrs Hornsby. Hadn't she donated a box of threads and an excess of wool to the church kneelers' cupboard?

"Only last week, that was," said Miss Moorcroft.

"Much better than tittle-tattling behind folk's backs."

The women nodded. Some were careful to avoid the betrayed faces of Miss Carstairs and Peggy Pinch, others delighted in watching their discomfort. The feeling was clear; the pair of plotters and schemers needed to be taught a lesson.

"We're being wafted aside," Miss Carstairs whispered to Peggy. They exchanged further disappointed glances when the postmistress declared that the group didn't have the skills to compete against St Faith's. Yes, they should complete one or two exhibition pieces but that shouldn't detract from the pressing need to replace those dozen kneelers that were threadbare. Miss Auboron, from White Gates, agreed. But the group had even more important matters to address, said the new chair. "We failed Janet McPherson. We didn't bring her into the fold."

"We don't know that she's been beyond bounds," said one woman with her head down. She stitched hurriedly. "Might well have done that Freddie Becker good. Mr Doughty from the old grocery was always wanting to be 'venturous but it was only the ne'er do wells who gave him opinions."

"Opportunities," someone corrected.

"You can't compare," said another.

"Anyways, he's dead these five and twenty years."

"I say there's those amongst us who wanted McPherson out from the start."

But no one pointed fingers and Miss Carstairs chose not to hear.

The group had been granted this open portion of the church floor because of the better light but it was a cold and draughty place. The women kept their overcoats buttoned up and several worked in knitted gloves with the fingertips missing. They wore hats and sturdy shoes, and each had a large needlework bag. These had been carefully made, although some were ancient with layers of repairs. The talk didn't dry up, yet one or two didn't say a word. Peggy always thought that the quiet ones enjoyed the gossip most.

As the three-quarter hour approached, Peggy withdrew to the pantry and, with an ear cocked and the door open, prepared two pots of tea with cups and saucers on a rickety supper trolley. No one spoke about her while she was busy; perhaps they thought Miss Carstairs was on guard.

"I've heard the doctor say that a position's to be found with an endowed school in town," said Mrs Willowby.

"That will be Margaret's," Miss Auboron surmised.

"Unlikely," muttered Miss Carstairs with her eyes elsewhere. No-one expected her to explain.

The new vicar's wife must not be discouraged in the same way, said the chair, and young Dorothy Becker would surely rebuild her confidence if she worked with the group each Wednesday. "Peggy, you're close. Perhaps you could have a word with her?"

"It's going well," Mrs Willowby said, already winding cottons and silks. She might have been talking about the amount of work done, but Postmistress Mary took the remark to be a congratulation on her chairmanship.

"Ethel Conlin kept our circle going so that we could mend such matters in the village. She wouldn't want us to be worried about competitions, the whereabouts of money or" – she paused to glance suspiciously at Miss Carstairs and Peggy- "who is elected chairman and who isn't."

The vicar had promised to close the meeting, so that the women could mark that good Ethel's spirit remained with them. When he failed to appear, Miss Carstairs said that it would be wrong for a lay person to lead a prayer in Reverend Nigel's church, so the circle sat in silence while each, in her own way, made peace with old Ethel.

As the group dispersed, the two conspirators wandered towards the church elm. "I never did like the woman," Miss Carstairs confessed. "Her circle is a lost cause, I'm afraid. Peggy."

"We must go alone," said Peggy. "We need a packet of mites' eggs."

"You must do nothing without me," ruled Miss Carstairs. "You've landed in trouble enough recently."

"A little mischief, that's all. Now, where would we find a nit's nest?"

The verger was known to be the enthusiastic angler in the village and had cultured most indescribables in his garden muck, but both women dismissed his name at once; he'd want to know what they were up to.

"Our peculiar professor knows all there is to know about creepy crawlies," suggested Peggy. "And he'd believe any yarn we spun."

"But he'd tell the others."

Peggy declared her favourite. "I trust Freddie Becker. I don't know how but he will come up with whatever we need. And it would do him good, knowing that he was trusted again."

Miss Carstairs stopped in the middle of the church path and, with both hands, clutched her handbag to her middle. "I'm worried."

"I know."

"I was your schoolmistress for eight years, Peggy Pinch. Didn't I instil the difference between right and wrong?"

"I say, something has to be done. That's all." Peggy said quietly.

"I know, I know. But I should discourage you from a night time naughtiness."

"But you agree it's for the best?" asked the policeman's wife. "Look, you're right. This is more my business than yours."

"No, I can't leave you to do it on your own." She made up her mind. "Besides, I am getting on, Peggy. How many more chances will I have to black my face? Leave Poacher Baines to me. I'll have it all arranged before midnight."

The pair recommenced their walk. "In the meantime, we've some detecting to do."

"Oh Peggy, dear. Isn't burgling St Faith's church enough?"

"But there's nothing uncertain about my idea. You're a member of the school board and I need us to examine the daily journals before Miss McPherson interferes with them or, worse, another member of the board takes possession of them. The third week in May, Rogation Sunday is important."

"You want me to unlock the headmistress's office?" She sighed, "Straightaway, then. We'll do it now and be done with it."

But Peggy held back. "There's something I've got to do first."

She delayed on the church green as Miss Carstairs' square, solid body marched down the village street. Queen O'Scots kept abreast on the other side of the road. Miss Carstairs had taught Peggy in school and, following the death of Peggy's parents too soon after the war, had kept an eye on her progress to womanhood. On Peggy's wedding day and during the week before, she had taken the part of the bride's mother. She was the only outsider who knew that the union hadn't been consummated for five years, and only fitfully since. She guessed there was no prospect of children and thought it a good thing. She also suspected that Peggy was spending too much time with someone else in the village, but she kept those thoughts to herself. The woman had a happy knack of knowing what to talk about and what to keep secret. Peggy supposed that they were best friends, although they never huddled in that way. Sometimes, Miss Carstairs' neighbourliness was all that made Arthur Pinch bearable.

CHAPTER FIVE

The Rescue of Baby Michael

It was half past twelve. Peggy had not been inside the police house since her early morning cycle ride. From twenty five yards, it looked a cold and wilting place, saddened by memories of an unhappy marriage. She stood in the middle of the lane, saying nothing to the three or four familiar faces that headed for the post office. The women would be there for forty minutes, celebrating that Peggy and Miss Carstairs had been put in their place. There would be much clutching of handbags as they complained that the vicar hadn't been where he should have been. But, really, the women were there for more spicy gossip, much of it peppered with innuendo about Peggy and Pinch.

She turned away, and wandered down the well-kept path to the open hut in the Beckers' back garden.

Ruby had promised her husband that her makeshift shop, with its dusty floor, wobbly displays and tattered second-hand posters, was more an insurance against the prospect of his unemployment than any makeweight for a clerk's low wages. Her sources were dubious. She had a jolly relationship with Poacher Baines and the neighbourhood tramp looked forward to trading goods of very uncertain provenance for a cup of tea and a warm in the shopkeeper's kitchen. The drayman, visiting the Red Lion twice a week, counted on Ruby taking in a box, if not two, hidden in a corner of his cart. But no one challenged the shop's legitimacy; it was evidence that the parish was looking after itself and Ruby's contribution to the village colour increased her say in what went on. The village growers who sold their surplus by scratching prices on slates, dug into their front verges, couldn't complain because Ruby's stock was far from run of the mill and, one by one, hadn't those gardeners passed their left-overs to her for a knocked down price?

Peggy was ready to ring the little hand bell when the back door to the cottage slammed and Ruby Becker came running up the path to serve her. "I saw you," she panted. "From the upstairs window, I saw you catching Becker on his way to work." Her face was drawn, the backs of her hands and her exposed ankles were red. She wore a housecoat and slippers. A screwed-up headscarf went from one hand to the other. She tapped her knuckles on anything she could find and her head jerked as her eyes sniped this way and that. The movement made her pointed face look even more like a chicken's than usual. "Mrs Pinch, you must understand how angry he is. He thinks that he's no way of protecting his children; who can blame him for being angry?"

"Have the police questioned him?" Peggy asked.

"No, why should they? He was with me in the church when Dorothy was messed with. We were in church and the children should have been in their bedroom. Oh my God! You mean questions about the murder. You think Becker did the killing? Mrs Pinch, how could you?"

"We have to accept that someone ..."

"No we don't! We don't have to accept anything! My Becker wouldn't kill anyone. Surely you know that. If not, then I'll tell you. He was in the vicarage when that women died. He finished work at one and went straight to the vicarage to work on the church accounts. You can ask."

"Has Dorothy said anything?"

"Only to my mother, though there's no sense in that. M'mam was dead three years before I had Dorothy. Do you want to know where I was?"

"Ruby, I didn't come here to question you. I'm sorry."

"And I don't want to fight with you. You don't want to buy anything in here, Mrs Pinch. Won't you come indoors for a cuppa? I've always thought that you and Dorothy shared things."

53

"I think we find it easy to talk with each other." Peggy pictured the hours before tea time when she and the young schoolgirl had sat on doorsteps, or on the war memorial bench, and swapped nuggets of wisdom in an unfair world. "I'm not sure who does better out of it. Being with Dorothy is very comfortable."

"I'd like you to try," said Mrs Becker. "Now that the house is empty and Becker is at work."

But as they left the wooden trading shed, the women saw Fisher's police Austin parked at the front of the post office. The detective pushed Baby Michael through the front doorway, his great hand clasping the suspect's shoulder.

"No!" shouted Ruby; Peggy clutched the flimsy sleeve of the housecoat to hold her from running forward. "But this is unfair!"

Postmistress Mary flung the bedroom window open and leant forward. "Leave him alone. He's done nothing wrong!"

The detective opened the car door with one hand and pressed down on Michael's head with the other, guiding him into the back seat.

The vicar had been knocking on the Beckers' front door. He quick marched towards their gate, mumbling meaninglessly, "No, no, no," then redirected himself towards Peggy and Ruby. "Ladies, do nothing."

"Go with him, reverend," Peggy pleaded. "Baby Michael has nothing to do with Ann Bidding's murder."

"But an hour in police hands will see him admitting to everything," said Ruby.

"Oh God, I wish Pinch were here."

"Mrs Pinch, I agree with you," said the vicar in two minds what to do. "We need a well rooted pair of hands. A man who's voice will carry."

"Do something," Peggy insisted, her teeth tight, her eyes smarting. "Can't Sergeant Fisher see what's plain in front of his face? He's completely wrong."

The motor car had already started up when the vicar crossed the street. He tapped urgently on the window. "Officer, may I travel with our Michael. He deserves caution, you agree. Advice and caution."

Already half a dozen villagers had gathered round. They were joined by the big men of the village – the cellar man, the verger and the roof-mender. Postmistress Mary ran from her house to her gate, then slumped on the grass verge and wrapped her face in her hands. She repeated her brother's name, over and over, through her tears.

"Do you not think that your duty is with those left behind, your reverence?" asked the detective.

Then came the strangest words. Michael leaned forward from the back seat so that his face was close to the open window. He said, "Don't worry, vicar. I won't tell on you."

"Oh, don't be foolish" Peggy said, quietly so that only Ruby Becker heard. "You've got to tell, Michael." She ran forward: "Michael! Everything is all right. Tell the detectives everything!" She was in the middle of the road when the police car began to roll forward. The vicar backed away while Peggy pursued the motor for half a dozen paces. "All right, Michael. It's all right to say what you saw!" Baby Michael's innocent face was at the little rear window, his fingers waving playfully like a child's.

Then the gears crunched and the car pulled into the side as the Thurrock's cart rattled from the ford at the bottom of the street. At the same time, Jones' boy was walking three heavy horses down from the top. A loose sheep wandered in from a twitchel and a worn out motorcycle, struggling to climb the hill, steered awkwardly towards the stationary police car and stopped. The rider, in a brown leather helmet, gauntlets and gaiters, was so anxious not to topple onto the bonnet of the official vehicle that he lost his balance and fell into the road. The sheep got between the motorbike and the car, three hairy horses blocked the road and Detective Fisher came out of the car in a temper.

"What are you doing, man!" he roared at the kneeling motorcyclist. "You with the sheep, get it out of here!"

Then he turned to his car and saw that his prisoner had gone. He stamped his foot. "Who's done that?"

Everyone in the assembly stood with their hands folded over their stomachs. No one risked a smile or a hint of satisfaction. The vicar pressed a little finger beneath his dog-collar, letting in some air, as he stepped forward. "Michael will wait for you in the vicarage. Wouldn't it be better to talk with him over tea and hot muffins?"

Fisher simmered. "You have broken the law if you've helped a felon escape, vicar."

Verger Meggastones allowed his principal no time to respond. "I pulled the lad from the car."

"Not without my help," added the cellar man.

"I laid my coat over his head," said a woman

"Me, too."

"Can you arrest us all, sergeant?" reasoned the vicar.

Fisher knew he was in trouble. He put his hands in his pockets and screwed a hidden handkerchief between his fingers. The station was expecting to receive the prisoner, but the prisoner had escaped because Fisher, contravening force orders, had come to the village alone. The rules said that two officers were required to arrest a man in foreseen circumstances. Fisher should have recruited a uniformed constable to assist him. He looked for a way out, but none of the twenty souls in the road was on his side.

"Vicar, I have no choice." He stepped forward hesitantly, ready to lay a hand on Reverend Nigel's shoulder.

The village could not believe that the detective was going to arrest their vicar. The lad, who had marshalled the horses along the opposite hedgerow, muttered, "Tain't lawful."

"There'll be a fearful row," Mrs Porter said, with no hint that controversy should be avoided. "You wait and see. Bishops and chief constables. Someone's mayor, I shouldn't wonder. I won't be surprised to hear the army's two pennyworth. The old colonel from Witchways; he knows a regulation or two."

Peggy managed to get alongside the detective. "The police house? I could write his name in the cell register and mark that he was paroled to the vicar's company."

"We'd need to list his property."

"I could do all that. Pinch isn't home, remember. No one will be the wiser."

"Mrs Pinch, I have made a bit of a mess."

She sighed. "The chief assigned you to this case when you've no

56

experience of working in a village. Country parishioners can be precious folk, Mr Fisher. Your mess will not surprise the chief constable."

The detective caught himself muttering, "It's what he wanted, all along."

As the downcast detective accompanied the vicar towards the church, with the verger and the cellar man not seven paces behind, he wondered just how much of a victim he was intended to be.

Dorothy Becker knew better than to show herself at the bedroom window but now that the cottage was empty she stood at the stairhead and listened to the commotion outside. She wore her nightie and slippers, and the dressing gown that hadn't been off her shoulders for two days. She knew that running away was her one way of making things better. She had brought so much that was wrong to those around her. Her house was in turmoil, a murder had been done, the post-lady was distraught because the police had come for Baby Michael and more trouble was waiting for poor Freddie. (He had slept on the floor of his parent's bedroom that night rather than in his bed in the children's room.) She needed to put matters right and all she could do was take herself out of the picture. The world would be good again, for everyone, if she ran away. When the Queen of Hearts had mocked her: "Running away to where?" Dorothy had answered, 'running away to heaven' and, from the moment that notion dawned, she knew that the brook and the water meadow was the best way to heaven. Water was the gateway.

She heard Mrs Porter and Miss Moorcroft shouting, Postmistress Mary was crying out loud and Mrs Willowby was telling Grace to go indoors. Only Peggy Pinch seemed to be looking for the truth behind what was going on. Peggy would be the one to help her. The policeman's wife had plenty of reasons to runaway away because, like Dorothy, no one really liked her. The policeman's wife – who always had time to listen, who had given her that first cigarette and stayed with her while she tried to smoke it, who came up with sayings that made sense and stuck in her head – would be the person who would guide her. As she listened, she recognised Peggy Pinch's voice in everything that the Queen of Hearts had said; so, after all, she had been testing her rather than teasing and taunting. Together, they would run away. Gosh, she was hungry; she wondered if she had time to secrete something from mother's pantry but she dared not risk anything that would spoil her running away plan. So, Dorothy went back to bed. She decided that they would do it tonight.

The good vicarages of England - where kitchen maids did less than they ought to do and gardeners knew more than they let on while the housekeepers knew less than they pretended, where vicars' wives were never properly on top of affairs and the men of these houses had the wisdom to make the best of things and settle for that - stood apart from other good buildings of the realm. It was often said, and Reverend Nigel agreed, that incumbents recognised that they held a vicarage in trust for their successors and often left behind parts of themselves, adding to the heritage and feel of the place but no man truly knew the history within the staid and incontrovertible walls of the parish castle. This was especially so in villages like Peg's where parishioners had been unhappy, over hundreds of years, with the priest chosen to take care of their heritage. Churchwardens exercised no say in the vicarage, bishops or their sergeants were either too easily contented or too willing to be fooled, and when did village policemen tramp around the upstairs corridors? Nigel thought that things might be different if the good vicarages of England had known, through the generations, more children.

Baby Michael, for example, was the only person who knew about the secret passage from the vicarage library to the second guestroom above. Peggy Pinch might say she had heard stories about it, and Mrs Frayle – at 93, the oldest soul in the village – might take her pipe from her mouth and say, yes, there is supposed to be something there but only Michael knew for sure. Only Baby Michael knew how to unlock the library passage and, more difficult, how to get out at the top. He knew about the floor safe in an unused cellar where, in his great grandfather's time, parish documents had been wrapped in cloth and stowed away – too precious to discard but too dangerous to be unearthed again. And, if he were ever asked, he could tell the real reason for the observation turret built at the back of the vicarage roof. The gardener liked to say that the old vicar used it for bird-watching but, no, Michael knew it was for nothing like that.

"This is a good vicarage," the vicar said as the three men settled themselves in the ladies sittingroom. "I've only been here a few months but I know it's a sound place, a safe place to talk, Michael."

Baby Michael smiled, feeling much better now, but he kept his secrets to himself. The detective was a stranger and had no business knowing about the secret passage and the cellar, and Nigel had not been here long enough to deserve to hear the ins and outs of his new home.

"You can tell Mr Fisher and me exactly what happened."

"Nothing happened," he said but too softly to be believed.

Fisher was still angry with the two men and unable to question his witness. He sat, as low as he could manage, in an armchair with his legs outstretched and his ankles crossed. He stared through the window, where the Peter Pan statue stood in the middle of the shallow pond and birds rested on the figure's head then fluttered away again. Here was a poor excuse for a policeman, the vicar thought.

"I was waiting behind the school for Janet," said Michael. "I was looking up from the footpath and she was at the staircase window. She had the children, you see, and couldn't come out to meet me. I was there for a long time."

Fisher allowed no indication that he was listening. To begin with, at least, Michael's account agreed with the woman's story.

"She did come down, just a few minutes before Mr Pinch's shout, and we spoke on the footpath. Reverend, she'd been very good to me, listening and such, and I wanted to spend a long time with her."

"So she was with you when the woman was killed, Michael?"

"I don't know when the woman was killed."

"She was with you before PC Pinch raised the alarm."

"We were with each other, sir."

"Michael, Sergeant Fisher needs to know how long you were waiting on the footpath."

"From one o'clock and until Pinch started yelling."

The vicar looked to the detective but the stony face gave nothing away.

"Did you see anything else?" the vicar asked.

"I saw the dead woman walking down the footpath, towards me, sir, and then she dipped into the twitchel. I suppose she came out at the war memorial and crossed the road to the Pinch's house."

"This was while you were waiting behind the school? She was alive after one o'clock? Think carefully, Michael."

"She followed me down as I was walking to the school. I don't know the time, do I. Exact times like that. When the church bell went, I was already at the school fence."

Fisher commented, "She saw Ann Bidding from the window, she says, between ten and five minutes to one."

"So what is wrong, sergeant?" the vicar asked.

"What is wrong is that Mrs Becker saw Janet McPherson on the banks of the bottom brook at one o'clock."

The vicar's wife came into the room and settled herself in the corner. She found some sewing beneath a cushion and busied herself, listening to every word as she stitched but saying nothing.

Fisher took up the interrogation. "You left the church in the middle of the funeral service and were missing at the time Dorothy Becker was attacked."

"That's wicked," Michael responded, "saying that I would hurt little Dot."

The Vicar intervened politely. "Sergeant, we all know that Michael went in search of his collie."

Michael slapped his knee. "Vicar, I can speak for myself. I'm fed up with people taking me for a baby. It's just a name, Baby Michael; it doesn't mean anything. I'm not backward. Mary leaves me in charge of the post office, doesn't she? And I've driven the bus before now. It's just at times, because people have never let me speak or think things out straight, I get fumbled. That doesn't mean I'm stupid."

There was an uncomfortable pause as Michael tried to remember the policeman's question.

"He had wanted to bring the dog into the church, sergeant," said the vicar. "But I gave way to Mrs Porter's complaining. I asked Michael to tie her up outside."

Mrs Fripps nodded and said, without looking up, "My husband means the dog, sergeant. Not Mrs Porter."

"I'd let her run free over the fields, so I went to the end of Wretched Lane and called her, that's all."

"So where were you when the murder was done?"

"That was the day after."

The detective repeated his question. "Where were you?"

Isabelle Fripps pricked her finger but kept her gasp to herself and searched her needlework bag for a thimble. 'He's already said he was with the school teacher,' she thought.

"Miss McPherson says you were with her but my chief saw you in the garden behind the post office."

"That was before," explained Michael. "I arrived on the bus from town. Mary had closed the post office and I knocked hard but got no answer, so I went to see Janet."

"But first, you spoke to the verger," said the detective. "The verger says you did."

"Yes but that was only for a second or two. I asked if he had seen Mary. He said no so I went to see Janet."

The detective unfolded his pocket book, licked the lead of his pencil and began to make notes. "Why?" he asked.

"Because I knew I was getting upset and Janet had promised to help me if ever I felt like that."

Fisher pushed further. "You gave her a cock and bull story about a women with stiff shoulders, a story you'd picked up from the lad Freddie."

"Sergeant, please," objected the vicar but Fisher raised a hand to stall him.

"It was true," Michael said, quietly but deliberately. "I did. I saw her. She was in the twitchel between Back Lane and the war memorial. I can't tell you who she was except that she doesn't live in our village."

"A mystery woman," the detective muttered incredulously. "A

61

convenient mystery woman that no one can identify."

"You've no reason to disbelieve him," said the vicar.

Belle lifted her head. "We'll sit together, Michael, and we'll draw a picture of her. You'll be able to help me, won't you?"

The witness nodded uncertainly. "She said, leave no witnesses to tell on you."

"Well that's ——"

"Wait, vicar. You must let me ask the questions."

"Michael has answered every one of your queries and my wife has offered to prepare a portrait of the most likely suspect. I think that is enough."

The detective uncrossed his feet. "I've given instructions for Miss McPherson to be released." The sounds of a busy vicarage intruded – the maid and the gardener were disputing rights in the kitchen and the hall clock was trying to strike the three quarter hour but the mechanism stuck. The Hoover was being worked upstairs. "There's little more to say."

Detective Sergeant Fisher knew that he had made a mess of things. He had come to arrest Baby Michael so that he could interrogate him harshly in the back room of the county police station, but the villagers had frustrated him from doing either. Worse, for Fisher, their closed ranks had demonstrated that any suspicions about the man were quite flimsy.

"I must visit the Willowbys," said the vicar as they walked along his garden path. "I'm afraid village affairs don't stop in the wake of a murder. If anything, they gather urgency." He tucked a knitted scarf into his coat collar. "I'm sorry if we've rather stood in your way this afternoon. I believe Michael is innocent, but you'll say that's because I want to believe him. He's not a daydreamer and he's not simple and his account makes sense. I cannot think of Miss McPherson having a stronger alibi."

"The mystery woman?" Fisher queried when he reached his car.

"A puzzle. My parishioners would love a mystery woman. Whoever she is, if she visited our village, I would expect twenty sightings and forty explanations. So, yes, she is rather a puzzle. I'm sure that my wife will present you with a more promising likeness but, at the moment, sergeant, you're looking for a woman with awkward shoulders."

"What did the lady look like?" asked the vicar's wife, adjusting her drawing board to make the most of the fading daylight.

Baby Michael, sitting on a dining chair close to her shoulder, with his hands in his lap and his ankles crossed, leaned forward: "A frog."

Her charcoal ran quickly over the paper. "A pair of hard set eyes at the top of her head, a snubbed sausage for a nose and a grin from ear to ear. Ears like your bruno bear, of course." She placed the frog at a pond's edge.

"Her mouth wasn't like that," he said. "It was open all the time."

"She breathed through her mouth." Her sketch was almost done. "That means that the sausage nose was a squashed sausage?"

Michael giggled. "Have you always been good at drawing?"

"I was the oldest child in our curate's school. He had to give his attention to the younger ones so he was happy for me to draw all morning."

"The church curate was head teacher?"

Looking back, a dispiriting number of people in Belle's childhood were curates or deacons or something similar. She said, "Our school was mornings only in the back room of the church and that wasn't on each Monday and Friday. In the afternoons, I was the egg maid. I wore a white smock and carried a wicker basket laid with straw. I listened carefully to the orders from the good wives of my village, then collected the right number of eggs from the cottages that kept hens. They were happy years but we worked hard. Mother took in sewing from town and made sure that I had plenty to finish off in the evenings. There." She sat back so that he could properly see Mrs Frog and her garden.

"Your village was like ours."

Oh, worse, she thought. Much worse. "Make fun of the lady's face, Michael."

She laid the frog to one side and started a cartoon to match Michael's mimicry. At once, he tilted his head to one side which Belle

Fripps thought was an important clue. The second picture took less than a minute but was as good as any in the newspaper funnies. Again, she placed it aside.

Drawing just as swiftly but more lightly, she began the more serious portrait. "Watch me closely and me put me right as I go," she said. But, as the portrait progressed, it seemed that the vicar's wife wasn't following Michael's instructions as closely she might have done. By stroke and smudge, she was subtly disguising the image.

"Anything else?" she sighed, scribbling her signature in one corner.

"Her Adam's apple was turned up, like a turned up nose in the wrong place."

Reverend Nigel had had little to do with the Willowbys of End Cottage. They were friends with the Beckers (the children were playmates) and Miss Carstairs had been a regular visitor during young Grace's recovery from the scarlet fever, but the Willowbys were a quiet family who minded their own business. "You've come about Gary," said Mrs Willowby as she welcomed him into the parlour. "Yes, thank you for sorting him out."

I've come about you, the vicar wanted to say but she had already withdrawn to make tea.

The grandparents were displayed on the table top. One set of frames was more elaborate than the other and the two branches were separated by a lace rose. Strange, thought the vicar, that there should be no wedding photographs or pictures of the children. It was as if the two families hadn't really come together. Mrs Willowby had put him in the best chair, in a corner away from the hearth but within easy reach of the tea tray. "Has Peggy Pinch been bothering you?" he asked.

"What a curious enquiry, vicar." She wore a floral pinafore with ribbon trim and so many ties that the vicar couldn't work out where they came from or where they went. She had the smallest hands in the village, he reflected. It wouldn't be many years before they began to shake.

"She called on you, this morning. I'm afraid our policeman's wife seems to be doing her rounds."

She poured two cups from the pot. "Things are so much better for us," she said. "Mr Willowby has found a job well within his capabilities, our Grace is coming out of herself, thank the Lord, and even little Gary is standing up for himself. I was so pleased when he argued with the postmistress."

"I've resolved the matter."

"So Gary says and thank you for the prayer book." She looked around and decided to sit on her daughter's stool. She kept her knees close together. "Mr Willowby sits with it in the evening, not that he says much about it."

"I'm afraid your husband and I have never really spoken."

"I think he would like you to call on us," she said uncertainly. "Sometimes, I don't think he gets what he wants from a church service. I'll see what he says and let you know." She went on stirring her tea, sighed and raised her eyes to look through the window. "Poor Dorothy's troubles have brought us closer to the Beckers. We always felt second-best, you know, Ernest Becker works in an office, Ruby makes herself useful with her little shop while we seem to be of no account. Even at play, Dorothy has been very hard on Grace and Freddie Becker will always be too much of a scallywag for my Gary to keep up with. But tones have changed, vicar. Very much changed and we thank goodness for it."

"I wonder," pondered the vicar, bringing his hands together until his fingertips touched in a cat's cradle.

"You wonder, vicar?"

"Would the Willowbys take over our little library? Miss Snagg made such a good job of it. When she died, we moved it to the vicarage annex and Miss Conlin was keen to run it for the village. But it's been sadly neglected with all that's happened."

Mrs Willowby's face brightened. "Yes, I could easily manage the hours and Mr Willowby could smarten things up. I mean, a little woodwork and paint. And Grace would love to draw some posters. Yes, vicar, the Willowbys would love to do it."

"Well, that's settled."

"I might pop up before tea. I'd like people to see that we mean business. We wouldn't want them to think that we're just talk."

For a moment, she seemed lost in thought.

"I could have a word, if Mrs Pinch has been a nuisance," the vicar said cautiously.

"Vicar, I invited Mrs Pinch for tea. It was my idea that she should come and see me. I wanted her to."

The vicar went "oh," and dipped his head, hoping for more.

"Tell me, vicar, are you worried about the policeman's wife or the Willowbys of End Cottage, because it seems to me that you are checking up on us?"

The vicar gave a modest cough. "I don't mean to … well, maybe that is what I'm doing. Checking up? Yes, I think I probably am but I'm more concerned about what is being said rather than who is doing the saying. Too many stories are being told. I'm afraid they will hurt someone, sooner or later."

"I'm so pleased to hear you say that. I've told Mrs Pinch that the gossips are spreading quite awful tales. Tell-tales of what was going on in her kitchen when that woman was murdered. Usually, I've no patience for such tittle-tattle but I thought she deserved to know. No one believes it, I've said that to Mrs Pinch. No one believes a word of it. I'm sorry to say this vicar, but I have heard that your wife is as keen as anyone to pass the stories on. Not that your wife's prittle-prattle is any of my business."

The vicar had been taught that it was a clergyman's privilege to keep quiet when they have nothing to say.

"I asked Peggy Pinch to call on me because I wanted her advice. There's a mention of a strange woman being seen in the village. I saw her, vicar. Just as we were ready to bury dear Ethel. It could only have been a couple of hours before poor Dorothy's ordeal. But it's not the time or place that bothers me. I am puzzled by something that perhaps only a woman could understand. That's why I haven't told the police. Outsiders, they always seem to write things down without really listening. Have you noticed that?"

"And what did you notice, Mrs Willowby."

"I was walking in Wretched Lane when she stepped out of the trees. She was adjusting herself, vicar."

"Yes?"

66

"Adjusting herself in the manner of a gentleman having convenienced himself."

The vicar showed his surprise. "And what did our constable's wife say to that, I wonder?"

"Well, that was odd. I don't quite know what she wanted me to do about it. She was very little help, I'm afraid."

"What did she say?"

"She said that she understood, vicar."

CHAPTER SIX

Janet McPherson's Story

Janet McPherson stopped her bicycle on the crest of the ridge so that she could watch the village, half a mile below. She had already drawn half a dozen sketches of the two lanes with their little cottages and she promised herself that she would start work on the tapestry, when all this nonsense was over. The church, its vicarage and the war memorial, the post office and police house, the school and the peculiar professor's lodge would make decorative reference points and she had some ideas for presenting Wretched Lane, at the top of the village, in ways that wouldn't give away its poverty. No one wanted needlework to show how bad things were. She would add some waterfowl to the brook and the ford and, though it would be difficult, she was determined to stitch the village bus in the distance. Originally, she had hoped that the tapestry would open some doors for her; the notion had been in her mind for almost a twelvemonth but the last two days had determined that she needed to get a move on.

Her school had been closed for the day. Tomorrow, she would sit down with the children and explain the reasons for her arrest. And her release. Old madam Carstairs would tut-tut at that (oh, how Janet could hear it in her head) but Janet McPherson believed that each child had a strength that could only be brought out through straight talking and responsibility. (If that meant she was too modern for a little village in England, so be it.)

She crossed the railway line where she shouldn't, then followed a bridle track across a corner of Thurrock's Farm. She meant to enter the village, unseen, through the overgrown gardens of Back Lane and the decrepit outhouses at the rear of the school. She needed to get out of these clothes. Then she needed to get into the village street. She would walk into the Becker's village store, dally in the post office, and sit reading at the war memorial before spending the evening in a corner of the Red Lion. She had steeled herself to wander and talk with the people whom she had avoided for so long. If the villagers were reluctant to talk, well, that was her own fault. But she had been ill, poorly of mind rather than anything else.

Since coming to her new neighbourhood, Janet McPherson's Scottishness had never been a problem. True, she had caught little Freddie Becker imitating her voice but she had the wisdom to make nothing of it. (Besides he had caught her soft Border accent so cutely.) But she had been more pained by the tail end of gossip that she had heard one day as she entered the post office. Mollie Sweatman spoke of the 'scrawny hen.' The ground was quickly covered up with coughs and splutters but the barb went home.

That afternoon, Janet had taken off every stitch and stood shamefully in front of a mirror. She was ashamed that she was standing naked before her own image and she was shamed by what she saw. Her first remedy was to eat more than she had ever done – potatoes, puddings, suet and sausages. She ate until her gluttony revolted her; then she showed penitence by making herself sick. The greediness was followed by abstinence. For days, she didn't eat bringing on faintness and a need to be sick when she couldn't manage it. This cycle - her trouble with nerves, she called it - kicked in whenever she felt fed up, anxious, taut or muddled.

She bowed her head to manage the well-trodden short cut through the professor's boundary hedge. Back Lane (or 'Bach' if you lived there) was the well to do side of the village with large residences - larger than the school, larger than the pub – with tall hedges to keep matters private. Miss McPherson was sure that sinful things went on in these houses. They sent their children away to school and kept them apart from the village children in the holidays less because they might catch disease or bad habits and more because their offspring might talk. Miss McPherson, alone in the village, invested her hopes in Ramsey McDonald.

The lane was empty when she crossed over and disappeared down the footpath, narrow and muddy, that led to the backs of her neighbours' homes. She recognised the children's voices in the brook, playing a rhyming game that had been in fashion for the past six weeks; it would soon be overtaken by Christmas chants. A travelling commercial had parked his van in the main street. She could hear Miss Moorcroft complaining and Mrs Becker asking for a stronger box. Out of their view, Miss McPherson hurried between the autumn trees and bushes.

Her progress stalled when she reached the rear boundary of the school property. She clearly saw Miss Carstairs and her crony, that irritating policeman's wife, going through her papers in the school office. She wondered if she should play cowboys and Indians, sneaking beneath the window where she might overhear their investigations. Tom Nix was the children's favourite. She had tried to inspire the girls with stories of Pocahontas but had yet to hear her name called in the playground.

But Janet decided not to spy. Polite timidity was the root of her problems in the village. Fools rush in might be a wise proverb but it was at odds with her renewed robust approach to difficulties.

She fished her key from her coat pocket as she marched across the yard, but the door was open. Making as much noise as she could on the nailed floorboards, she stomped along the short corridor, past the portraits of old governors and benefactors, and opened her office door.

For long moments, none of the three women spoke.

Peggy, so often caught out of bounds, broke the stalemate. "We're on your side, Janet. We need to know when you first noticed that Bredon's Parish Records was missing, that's all. We would have waited but who knows how long the police intended to keep you."

"The book of breakages," Miss Carstairs suggested.

Janet McPherson left the room without a word.

Miss Carstairs was sitting at the desk where she had spent most of her working life. It was impossible not to be drawn to her yesterdays. She thought of the quiet moments in this office when she had opened the bottom drawer of the desk and returned to the photograph of her lost love. The afternoons when she had worried about the damp patch on the wall behind the two document cupboards. The many problems that had been resolved by sitting here and talking to worried parents.

In the few moments before Janet returned, she said, "You must do the talking, Peggy. If I speak, we'll argue."

Janet came back with the well-worn pocketbook. "I was checking poor Freddie's buttocks for impetigo. You would have done the same." She handed over the book for inspection. "Here is the entry about the missing book. I wrote a note to the board on the same day."

'I would have called the nurse, or even the doctor,' Miss Carstairs said in her head. Her prejudice against the new mistress wouldn't concede that such steps would have led to trouble with Ruby and Mr Becker.

"How could I know that he would do the same to his sister?"

"You should know your children," Miss Carstairs commented and immediately wanted to swallow her words.

Janet McPherson was angry, but kept her own counsel. "And I don't believe, for one moment, that he did anything more to Dorothy than I had done to him. The doctor has told me how the little lady suffered and I'll swear before anyone that young Freddie wouldn't have abused her in that way."

Peggy fingered through the record book; it confirmed her theory of the book thefts, "Why weren't you with the rest of us at Ethel's funeral?" she asked quietly.

She nodded to the woman at the desk. "She knows."

"Baby Michael's been questioned."

"Baby Michael is nothing to do with anything. He was with me when that woman was murdered."

"You arranged to meet?" Miss Carstairs asked.

Peggy wanted Miss Carstairs to keep quiet. Her voice was barbed, as if she were seeking out scandal.

"I was trying to help him," Miss McPherson explained. "His heart is broken, Mrs Pinch, you know that. And when poor Dorothy was attacked, he was waiting for Poacher Baines at the end of Wretched Lane. That's why he left the burial service early."

71

"You're sure about that?" continued Miss Carstairs.

"That's what he's told me and he doesn't know how to lie."

Miss Carstairs rose from the chair. "Come on, Peggy. We'll leave by the front door."

Janet McPherson didn't follow at first. She called after them, "You've no right to be on the board. Think you can just walk in here and go through my things, do you?"

As they marched through the corridor and out of the school, they heard her bringing her desktop to order. But they hadn't made the school-gates when the woman came running across the quad.

"You two busybodies are the worst in the village!" she shouted. "No one here likes you. You think you know everything and what's in people's head but ..."

Miss Carstairs rounded on her. "Don't you start on me, you young viper!"

Peggy gripped her friend's sleeve, pulling her through the gates and into the village street.

But Janet McPherson's resentment was beyond boiling point. "You're nought but an ol' dragon! Let people see you are! Come on, then!"

The two schoolteachers were in the middle of the street, twenty-five yards apart and daggers drawn. Miss Carstairs – stout, well wrapped up and over sixty. Janet McPherson - thin and scrawny, cold-looking and less than thirty. Neighbours came out of doors, working men downed tools and stepped forward to watch. Some bunched a few yards from the younger one, just as many were ready to catch the older if she broke down. But many more lined the narrow lane, treading on the verge, leaning on fences and gates or hiding behind hedges.

"I've seen you," McPherson was shouting, "creeping into my school in the middle of the night, nosing into what I've been doing and going through the stores. You've always been against me."

"You're stifling our children. Can't you see, this is a school in their village, not somewhere where they go to march in twos and stand in squares?"

"They love coming to my school. Do you see them, wanting to

stay away? Not even at harvest time, they don't. I've read your old journals when they all stayed away."

"You're introducing the little ones to French. Where's a purpose in that?"

When Peggy, having stepped aside to the grass verge, prayed aloud, "Dear God, we've got to stop this," she felt a hand on her elbow.

Reverend Nigel, in dog-collar and tweeds, whispered, "In these circumstances, time is the only healer. We must let things take their course."

Peggy turned to face him with tears for an old friend heavy in her eyes. "You don't understand."

"You changed things for the sake of cha ——"

"I have not! I have deliberately left things in place so that you can be remembered. For God's sake, you old crow, look at how I've kept your memory in place." She clenched her fists at her sides and yelled: "I know what you did for the place, and y'can still do so much, but for pity's sake, let me in!"

Three or four, no more, clapped at that but they soon gave way to Carstairs' bellow. "Then don't shut me out!"

The village roofer, with thatch in his hair, took one step forward and without lifting his voice, offered, "Where are the children in this? Do you see them wanting to take sides?"

"Teaching them French, they'll know more than their parents," grumbled Mrs Porter.

"Can't see much bad in that," said the cellar man. He hitched his britches. "Deserve a sight better than we're gi'ing them this last month."

Then, at once, everything stilled. The yapping stopped and each stony-faced figure kept to its place. Eyes were fixed on the boy messenger, no older than fifteen and soldier-smart in his post office uniform, who was bicycling slowly up from the ford. A telegraph cadet rarely brought good news. Sometimes a visitor would send on ahead, giving the time of their arrival but that was rare these days. More often, a telegram meant that more sorrow was ready to fall on one of the cottages. Young Cecil had been to the village before and knew the address he needed. He stopped in the middle of the road, the toe of one shoe on the ground keeping him steady. "It's for Miss McPherson," he said as he drew the folded flimsy from the leather purse on his belt.

The Scots mistress swayed backwards and would have fallen if Verger Meggastones hadn't been standing behind her. The vicar's wife stepped forward, taking hold of the message. Everyone watched as she ripped open the perforated edge of the paper.

"Your mother's in Cardiff Infirmary," she relayed quietly.

Janet McPherson eyes closed.

"Can't be," someone whispered. "Cardiff's not in Scotland. It's a mistake."

Miss Carstairs fell in with Belle Fripps, "Let's get her inside," and the two women, with Mrs Porter behind them, supported Janet towards School Cottage. "The children," Janet kept saying. "What about the children?"

"They'll be fine," said Miss Carstairs. "I'll speak with Doctor Bolton. I'm sure he'll arrange for someone to come over from St Margaret's."

"No, I want you to take school in the morning. They'll need to see someone they know." But her words seemed bewildered and distant.

Strong tea, the colour of roasted chestnut, a rug for her knees, a shawl around her shoulders and an extra log on the fire brought some colour back to her face. Mrs Porter rubbed the woman's hands.

Now was the time for the older women of the village to play their part as, item by item, they dealt with the likely distractions. Yes, Miss Carstairs would look after the school but nothing would be changed; each day would run as Miss McPherson intended and when she came back she would find that everything was the same. Her two rooms, at the back of the school, would be kept aired but no one would nose around. The little kitchen would be brought up to stock.

"But I'm street monitor, this week."

"No matter," the others said.

Because the telegram had spelt the worst, the women didn't speak of medical miracles or hospitals being the best place for the sick. Instead, the business was to get Janet there in time. A message had been sent for Driver David to get the village bus working. Mrs Porter would see her safely on the train.

Miss Carstairs was working on the railway timetable. "You can manage across London?"

"I can travel that far with her, if needs be," Mrs Porter assured everyone.

Miss Carstairs was turning the pages of the ABC Guide. "You will have to change again at Swindon. Fortunately, I've a cousin. I'll telephone ahead so she'll be on the platform to help you with the connection."

Miss Carstairs and Mrs Porter, who weren't on speaking terms, were working together with a neighbourliness that might have fooled a stranger into thinking they were friends.

These were village matters. "Janet, you must remember that your best friends are here," said the vicar's wife. "We'll let no one intrude." If the police asked, they would be told where she was and told to keep away. "Mrs Pinch is making up a picnic basket for you. She won't be long."

Before the teapot was finished, there was a knock on the door and young Grace Willowby, quite the most grown-up of the parish offspring, was brought into the parlour. "Everyone helped as best they could," she said handing over the collection. "Mother says there's no one who didn't give. She hopes it's enough for the train journey."

"Oh, I couldn't."

"You must," insisted Mrs Porter and Miss Carstairs allowed no more to be said about it.

The Willowby child stood in the middle of the women, each old enough to be her grandmother and more. "I'm to bring some patties down from Mrs Killings, she says, just as soon as they're done and the doctor is ready to run you to the station. Would you like me to come with you? I'd be someone to talk to."

Her schoolteacher smiled. "No, no. You must help Miss Carstairs tomorrow and visit Mrs Becker so that Dorothy knows you're ready to sit with her when she's ready."

Grace promised.

"You will show Miss Carstairs what we've been doing with the nature table, won't you?" Then she allowed an edge to her accent. "I want no little tyke getting away wi' things."

CHAPTER SEVEN
The Chief Intervenes

The chief constable had been digging the wet ditch for forty-five minutes and, although progress was slow, every shovelful convinced him that his strategy was right. On the face of it, an armoured train on the branch line provided the best defence of the mound but the chief was concerned about an attack from the east. His trick would be to entice the invader onto the marshy ground below him so that this could be turned into a killing field. A short ditch, fifty yards below the line of the crest, was the best way of achieving this. He had allowed himself no rest. His joints felt free, his limbs felt stretched and, though he wasn't without aches and twinges, his back felt good. A good back was the prerequisite of every hands-on engineer.

When a far-off church tolled four, the chief climbed his bank of debris and surveyed the shallow vale of farmland. The autumn light was already failing. "Good stuff," he mumbled.

Fisher had parked the police Austin where the county lane was sheltered by four broken trees. The chief watched him dip and stumble as he tried to cross the field. He was using his arms to break any fall rather than to balance and propel himself. "Utter duff," grumbled the chief and dropped back into the ditch. "The man's no idea. No ideas at all."

"The middle clue had me foxed," the young detective shouted when he was thirty paces off, "until I realised that it was code for a map reference."

The chief put extra gumption into his digging. He even grunted for effect. "You stayed in the car for ten minutes. Why did you do that? I don't understand why."

"I was writing up, sir."

"Bit of an interruption, am I?"

"I was on my way to interview Mrs Pinch but not at all, sir. Sir, might I …"

"'May I' would be more courteous. If you are going to risk impertinence, you should always go for the softer tone. Khartoum, Fisher? Have you ever studied the defence works of Khartoum? No? Then, you should. Gordon is well remembered as a man of God but, at heart, he was always an engineer. That's what made him a genius."

"Khartoum, sir?"

"I was speaking to John Buchan, just a twelve-month ago. He was lecturing to young journalists and, afterwards, I said to him: Khartoum. Like minds, Fisher. We're men of like minds."

Fisher couldn't fathom why he was standing in a farmer's field, talking to his chief who, it appeared, had wasted an afternoon digging a trench in someone else's ground. "I've had to let the postman go," he said.

"He's no postman, Fisher. He's the postmistress's brother and of course you must release him. He has nothing to do with the matter."

"He gave the schoolteacher an alibi."

"Which one?"

"The Scottish one. He said, he had agreed to meet her behind the school sheds. She didn't turn up, but he saw her at the top windows of the school. Saw her plainly, he said, at the time the killing was done."

"Fisher, have you studied the mission close to Sally-Wanda?"

Fisher stared, bewildered, at the chief's craggy face. "Miss Wanda, sir?"

"The battle, Fisher, of Sally-Wanda. Bloody massacre in the Zulu wars. But the defence of the mission hut is a lesson well learned."

"I've had to release them both. Baby Michael and the Scots Mistress."

The chief was furious that his subordinate wouldn't take the history lesson. The man was supposed to be leading a murder enquiry but he had no direction, no strategy, and no foresight. The chief stuck the shovel deep in the ground, then levered it until the wet mud squelched. "Why is he called Baby Michael?"

"Baby, sir? He just is."

"Just is! Just is! What sort of policeman says 'Just is'?"

Fisher persisted. "It's a matter of building a picture of where everyone was at the important time."

"Don't complicate the case, Fisher. The parents have the best motive, don't they? Ann Bidding was in the woods when their daughter was molested. No-one else in the village had a reason for murder, except the parents, Fisher. Except the parents. Do you know of anyone else in the village who knew the woman?" The cold wind nipped at the chief's ears, turning the tips red. He bared his teeth and sucked in; he had always believed that cold fresh air was the best way of cleaning them. "Well, do you? Of course, you don't."

"I want to talk to you about that, sir. You see, there's yourself."

"Myself, man!"

"You did know her, sir, and you were on the scene just minutes before the body was found."

"Grief, man!"

"Not wanting to complicate the case, sir, but I need to know ..."

"Need to know! Then, I'll tell you. I left Pinch's garden at ten minutes before one o'clock. The onion shed was locked but, yes, Pinch unlocked it, I remember. He wanted to show me the insides. I said I didn't have time so he closed the shed door and, I'm sure, he didn't lock it. I walked up the village street, intent on discussing the wayward child with her vicar. I spoke to the maid, who went to see the vicar's wife, who wasn't there, and when she came back she said that the vicar was out on his rounds."

"Rounds, sir?"

"I'm relieving you of the investigation, Fisher. You've arrested two people who could not possibly have murdered Ann Bidding and you're no nearer understanding the case. The parents are in the middle of this, mark my words. Or the vicar. Don't trust the man.

79

Strange ideas on his calling. But then, I doubt you've even spoken to the fellow."

"I'm off the case, sir?"

"Maddocks will make a far better job of it. Go back to the station, young Fisher, and place your writings-up on Mr Maddocks' desk. Dismissed, Albert Fisher, dismissed."

PART TWO

CHAPTER EIGHT
They Walked by Night

At eight o'clock, the mist came down, chilly enough to stick to the ends of noses and turn cheeks red. The children were cold in their beds. The Willowby ones whined and demanded but, next door, the Becker pair persevered, though their suppertime soup had hardly been thick enough to fill their tummies. Across the road in tiny Rose Cottage – now only half as wide as it had been intended – three years old Alexander knew what to do on a cold night. He skipped into his mother's bed, knowing that she would come up when she was ready; this house knew no father.

By ten o'clock, Driver David was out of doors, dressing the bus engine and hoses with makeshift lagging. Verger Meggastones had promised to patrol the main street at eleven because Pinch wasn't there to complete his best walk of the day. But it was so cold and bleak that he spent his first forty-five minutes in the Red Lion kitchen.

"I heard the parson talking to young Willowby," said the landlady. "Tell him from me, the lad makes a good paperboy."

"Goodnight verger!" laughed the roof-mender as he cycled up the lane, his back wheel squeaking with each rotation and his bell tinging haphazardly. The noise made a macabre toll that became slower and slower as he climbed the hill. "Saw you on the thatch, I did, verger! A good use of fleece shears!" He let out a mocking laugh.

"Goodness. I didn't know our voices carried like as much," Meggastones said.

Ten minutes later, Peggy Pinch – crouching at her bedroom

83

window so that she could peep unseen through the curtains – saw the verger's broad shape emerge from the drifting mist. He walked through her front gate and established himself on the porch below her. He pulled a pipe from his pocket and got it going with a couple of puffs of an experienced smoker. She knew he would be there for twenty minutes.

Few things annoyed Mr Pinch more than this habitual trespass by his gardening rival.

'The bugger's not here to pinch secrets,' he would say. He rarely used bad language in front of his wife, but the antics of Meggastones merited exception. 'The bugger's here to listen on us.' And, no doubt, the fat verger had learned more about the tribulations of the Pinch marriage than most citizens of the village.

Keep quiet and do nothing, Peggy told herself, and he'll be gone before midnight. She only hoped that Miss Carstairs had noticed the spy; if she came out of Old School Cottage while he still stood sentry, their game would be up.

As he got to the end of his pipe, he coughed, cleared his throat, and struck another match to make sure that every last shred of tobacco had burned; the sign of a dirty smoker, Pinch liked to say.

"You there, Peggy Pinch?" came his gruff voice. "I know you'll be listening to me. Show your face, woman, so as we can talk proper."

Peggy kept low.

"They'll be talk if I come to your back door," he warned. He was packing his pipe for a second time and wouldn't speak until he was smoking again.

Peggy opened the window and pushed her head out. He was hidden beneath the porch and, all the time that he stayed on the step, neither of them would have the angle to see the other's face.

"Just what do you think you're up to, Verger Meggastones, trespassing where you're not wanted when you know my husband's not about to see you off?"

"I don't mean to trouble the old fool. I've come to pester his wife."

"You've a vulgar tongue, verger, and you think the dark will

84

cover up your mucky manners. Please, count on me telling him when he gets back."

He took his pipe from his mouth. "Things is wrong, Peggy Pinch, and not talking about them won't put them right."

Peggy folded her arms on the window frame and pushed herself forward. Still, she couldn't see him.

"The children aren't talking, that's what particular to our circumstances. Dorothy Becker's lost her wits. Her bro' Freddie has already said enough to be in trouble and won't risk telling more. Gary Willowby knows most, I reckon, but nobody's asking him and lovely Grace is speaking to no one but old Madam Frayle. We know why that is, don't we? The young mademoiselle knows the ancient has got no time for the rest of us. What she says to Elsie Frayle is as good a secret as a child can make. You know what I think? I think the young ones have got hold of an aspect that the rest of us is blind to. And, like all guilty knowledge, they don't know what to do with it."

"An aspect, Mr Meggastones?"

"An aspect, Peggy Pinch."

She caught the smell of his pipe as the smoke curled and grew into the night air. Meggastones' choice was a sweet mellow tobacco that burned too quickly for popular taste. Pinch, always ready to do his rival down, called it burn for a lady's pipe. The copper also promulgated the slander that he soaked his spare bowls in honey harvested from Edna Thurrock's hives. (The verger was known to spend time at the rich woman's farm.)

"The aspect, madam, of why. Why was the woman killed?"

Peggy didn't want to join in his conversation. She wanted to send him away, leaving the coast clear for her own escapade. But she answered him. "Because she saw what happened to poor Dorothy."

"Now, you and I, Peggy Pinch. You and I know that, whatever was done, was done by Freddie, not that I attach any evil intent to the lad. Experimenting, I'd say. Likely as not, experimenting on both their parts. No one thinks our Freddie could kill a grown woman, making such a blood-ridden job of it. Nonsense, Peggy Pinch, as well you know it."

85

"Verger, this is neither the time nor the place for discussion."

"I cannot think of a better time, Peggy, but I'm sure we'd do better in your scullery. I've always had a fancy for you, I'll not deny it."

"You're a rude and scandalous old goat! You think I'm an easy woman who takes callers in the middle of the night when her husband is away? I'll be sure to tell Mr Pinch of your ambition."

He took the pipe from his mouth. "Now, what's that Carstairs woman doing, leaving by her back path and taking the twitchel in the direction of the church. Has she got special prayers, d'you think? Prayers too guilty to say in bed?"

Peggy bit her lip. Now, rather than sending the verger away, she needed to distract him until Miss Carstairs was out of the way.

"This time of night," he continued, "you would think she'd walk up the lane rather than the treacherous footpath. She needs to be careful not to trip." He slipped the hot pipe in his coat pocket and was ready to step forward from the path, when Peggy slammed the bedroom window with a clatter.

The verger was waiting on the stone step when she opened her back door.

"Don't take your coat off," she said, but he was already draping it over the back of a wooden chair.

"Sit down and don't move," she instructed. "I won't be lighting the ring so late. You'll get no tea."

"But you can't begrudge a man his hot oats on a night like this. Come on, Peggy. Mrs Becker has acquired a full sack for nothing at all, and I'm sure you'll have stowed a jar in your pantry."

She filled the kettle and put it on the stove with plenty of noise, hoping that said how angry she was. She held her tongue while she boiled the water and mixed the drinks in beakers. Then she sat opposite him: "Let's be having you," she said. "You know why the murder was done?"

He shook his head. "I know the path to take." He hadn't touched his drink. "I like to stir my tea while I'm drinking."

Peggy rapped two knuckles on the table, got up, fetched a spoon from her drawer and slapped it in front of him. "No more of your nonsense," she warned.

Verger Meggastones wasn't a man to be told. He lived alone. He decided his own day, doing little by habit and using his parish appointment as a licence to poke his nose where he scented intrigue or betterment. There wasn't a busy housewife in the village who knew what was going on better than Verger Meggastones. He told the vicar what was right and wrong with his church, altered the church diary with little warning and practised a knack of making sure that parish moneys moved along paths he had prepared. He was a good man, people said, but he liked to provoke. His rivalry with Pinch amused everyone. The pair fought over public works and drainage, village trees and gardening. Red Lion drinkers knew that either would disagree with the other over anything or nothing, but it was unusual for a day to pass without their sharing half an hour together. The true depth of their friendship was difficult to fathom but, without doubt, it had been moulded over several years and had guided the village through many tribulations. Peggy was sure that sitting in her kitchen after midnight was part of his game; it put him one up on the village bobby.

"Going no further than what we know," he said, sipping and then stirring, "no soul in our village had reason to murder Ann Bidding."

"She was a stranger to us all." Peggy closed her eyes and shook her head. "That means Freddie is the only one with a motive but I can't ..."

"Neither can I. Nothing will convince me that young Master Becker has anything to do with this butchery. No, Peggy. Peggy, we need to go further than what we know."

Peggy understood. "Someone amongst us knew Ann Bidding of old."

Meggastones finished his drink with one great mouthful and placed his beaker heavily on the table top. "No other version explains it," he said.

"They've done well to keep it quiet. The village has much that's unsaid but little that's unknown."

"We've newcomers, Peggy. Figures who had lives beyond our little parish, outside of our history. Each will have reasons for coming here."

"Janet McPherson," said Peggy.

"The vicar and his wife," said Mr Meggastones.

"Our Doctor."

"Your husband's chief constable. Why has he such a presence in the case?"

"Enquiries in our little world won't bring out those secrets. We'd have to set some sort of trap."

The verger's rugged face stretched to a smile. "And no one better for that than our policeman's wife." He checked his pocket watch. "Time well spent, I make it. Tell me, do you have some of Pinch's favourite almond toffee."

Peggy glared suspiciously. The man knew that the flask was kept on the top shelf of the dresser and Peggy would need to climb two or three steps to lift it down. (It was Pinch's tease to stow it beyond her convenient reach.)

She took a ring of keys from their hook and opened the door to the little cell block. "The doctor has extended his practice from St Faith's," she said, stepping over the laundry which she had parked in the cold passage. "I'm sure we already know all that we need to know about him. Doctors find it very difficult to keep their secrets, you know." She extricated some folding steps from a pile of mops and brooms. As she carried them into the scullery, she said, "Mr Meggastones, please don't think I don't know what you are up to."

Carefully arranging the steps where she knew they would wobble, she asked him to stand by in case she tumbled.

"The school board looked carefully into Miss Janet's background," she said. "But such checks can never be certain."

She climbed to the third step and, leaning against the middle shelf of the dresser, bent one knee, raising her skirt to reveal the length of calf that the verger wanted to see. "The bishop will know everything about Nigel and Belle Fripps, but if I'm to make headway with the bishop, I shall need to be very clever."

At the right moment, she shifted her weight so that the steps shuddered and she jumped rather than fell. The big verger caught her and suddenly their faces were close. His pale blue eyes, which should have been soft and comforting, were scary on such a tough face. Then

88

she felt the pressure of his hand against the back of her thigh.

Trying a trick that she had seen Pinch work more than once, she pulled herself free, dipped aside and came up again behind him. Before he had time to turn, she reached through his legs, grabbed the front of his trousers and pulled back hard.

He gasped, and when he crouched forward, she kicked his fat seat and sent him down the single step to the little passage to the cells. He reached for the doorframe of the open cell, pulling himself to his feet. But he was in too much pain to stand straight. Peggy grabbed the front of his shirt and, with all the deliciousness she deserved, she slapped his whiskered cheek.

"Bitch," he spat, wiping a trickle of blood from the corner of his mouth to the back of his hand.

Peggy saw that he was still unsteady on his feet. She drew her hand back and, clenching her fist at the last moment, summoned all the power in her shoulder to throw a punch to his fat twisted nose. This time, he didn't catch his breath or cry out. His face shot sideways. She thought she heard his neck crick. As he was falling backwards, she gave one more, unnecessary, kick and told him what she thought of him.

Plump Verger Meggastones measured his length on the cell floor. Peggy didn't wait. She slammed the cell door and turned the heavy key in the lock. He hadn't made a sound.

She put her ear to the door. She didn't hear him moving. "If you keep quiet, I shall have you out of here before daylight." No noise at all. "If you make a fuss, I'll make sure people know what you came here for."

Now, she hesitated. She wondered if she should open the cell door and tend to him. But Verger Meggastones was too fond of playing tricks on her. "You've won, Peggy Pinch," she whispered to herself. "The man got what was due. Don't spoil things by being kind."

It was time to get a move on. The neighbourhood poacher had set a strict timetable and Miss Carstairs was already out of doors. Dress for the night, they had both insisted and Peggy went from room to room, gathering the clothes that would make up her costume. Twice, she returned to the cell block and twice she refused to give in to Meggastones' teasing. She was sure that he was keeping silent as a temptation to open the door. She gave in to knocking on the heavy wooden panels and speaking quietly to him. "Are you all right, verger? Stay quiet and I'll open you up before breakfast." He gave no reply; he gave not even a stir.

The empty church was cold and unlit. An accident of moonlight allowed the shrine of St Agnes to look down on the chamber from a corner enclave, reserved in the olden days for the squire and his family. Queen O'Scots prowled around the font, alert for any scent of a church mouse. Peggy Pinch, who had come to the church only after checking that every light had been extinguished in the vicarage, stood up from her prayers, curtsied before the alter, then, avoiding the aisle, stepped down the edge of the church. Not for fear of being seen but because footsteps didn't echo so much along the side walls. She was dressed in her husband's gumboots, a pair of a policeman's trousers (so baggy on her that she employed a second pair of his braces), and a uniform tunic that reached down to her thighs. She wore the black hat that she had worn at Ethel Conlin's funeral. Miss Carstairs had suggested that they should soot their faces but Peggy thought that was going too far.

The retired school-ma'am was waiting in the porch. In less than twelve hours, she had purloined some discarded black curtain liner from the school cupboard, cut and stitched it into a pair of loose trousers and a free flowing jacket.

"You look like a Peking woman," Peggy remarked.

"Indeed." She produced a dark head-square to complete the picture of Madam Wishy-Washy. (Miss Carstairs did feel like a pantomime horse.) "You've got the mites' eggs?"

"More than enough."

"Then let's get going."

Their squat bulky figures, shaped like wicked crows in the night, crossed the graves and left the churchyard by rolling over the low stone wall. Without a word, they trudged along Wretched Lane to the edge of the village. It was a quarter to one.

Poacher Baines didn't show himself until he was sure the women had neither been followed nor observed. Then he came out of the hedge, stepping in their way, and gestured that they must become his shadow and talk only in sign language. Peggy's first thoughts were that he was done up for the wild frontier, with his rabbit skin cap, a criss-cross of belts hanging from his shoulders, trusted fur-lined boots and two trapper's coats. After a hundred yards, she was horrified to work out that the contraption on his back could be turned into a lethal cross-bow.

Without a word, the curious troop disappeared into the woodland. Baines kept away from the regular footpaths and well-trodden shortcuts. In no time, the wet had seeped into Peggy's skin, and Miss Carstairs' legs were scratched and grazed but their slow, step-by-step progress didn't falter.

When Miss Carstairs had recruited the poacher, she had emphasised that while, in weeks to come, many wives of St Faith's might suspect that their neighbouring parish might have been up to some sabotage, the truth must never be detected. It was, she had repeated with an earnestness which amused, a most dangerous escapade.

Baines knew how to stay out of gaol. Traditionally, he kept the village on his side by delivering small game to its tables. And buttering-up the local bobby by hanging a hare or pheasant on his door was a tradition that he had learned as a boy. But he was ready to see the advantage of drawing the policeman's wife and one of the most influential parish voices into his circle of allies. They would learn nothing about him.

Peggy tried to keep her sense of direction but the little party turned back on itself so many times that, soon, she had no idea where she was. Just as, two nights before, Dorothy had looked for the noble oak and the unjumpable ditch as she fled through the woods, Peggy expected to see these familiar landmarks from her childhood. It was in these woods that she had first seen Pinch, chopping down a tree. But the poacher kept the women away from anything they could mark. Sometimes Peggy thought that they were retreading their steps but she showed no surprise; they trudged on.

He didn't rest them until they reached the crest which marked the edge of the woods. The church of St Faith's slept at the foot of the valley. He allowed them to look before silently indicating that they still had a mile and a half to go. Then, suddenly, he signalled them to crouch down.

A shift of light showed Miss Carstairs' worried face. Peggy edged close to her. She had a story ready if they were detected at this stage, an easy story for no one would believe that two respectable women were part of a night-time poaching expedition. She whispered, "Better be caught here than St Faith's."

When the old poacher scowled at her breaking the silence rule, Peggy lowered her eyes in contrition. She couldn't believe that anyone was about, ready to call for their arrest. Who would be here at this time of night?

They lay on the ground for long dreary minutes, before their guide encouraged them to peer through the long yellow grass. Faraway, the lights of a motorcar was crossing the landscape and a carter was manoeuvring beneath the lamps of Thurrock's farmyard, but they would not bother them. Then he indicated the steam locomotive, stationary at the old signal box two or three miles distant. Tapping his sleeve, knocking his forehead and running fingers up the sleeve of his coat, he told them that the driver wouldn't move for twenty minutes. But, again, that wouldn't interfere with their progress, Peggy thought.

Then she realised that he had assembled his crossbow with practised agility and was concentrating on the thicket to their left. Absolute silence, he demanded. She could neither see nor hear his quarry but watched the studied patience on his craggy face. He aimed, relaxed and comfortable.

She heard the flight of the bolt and the puff of air as it punctured flesh. She heard the creature sit back on his hind legs but still she couldn't work out where or what it was.

The old shoulders dropped and Baines drew an arm across his forehead. "Keep to the hedge, all the way down. Folk in the village will be able to make out your shapes if you stray towards the path. Don't be tempted. When you reach the crossing, go wary. Listen hard. Don't stare into the night but let your eyes drift so that they can catch any movement at the edge of their capture. I'll shall be here until three o'clock to guide you back home. If you fail to make the point, you must find your own way. If that's the case, don't trust yourselves in the woods but follow the lanes the long way round, with a good story ready if you're challenged."

The women obeyed and covered another half mile before Peggy spoke.

"I think it was a deer."

"We know nothing about it," Miss Carstairs mumbled, her head choked with misgivings.

"I'm sure he shot it in the throat."

"We know nothing about it."

Peggy sensed that her mentor was losing heart and would readily agree if Peg suggested giving up. Practical jokes and sabotage were against the old school-ma'am's nature. Peggy knew that she was taking part because she had been piqued by the smug attitude of the church kneelers and the fun the circle had found in isolating her and Peggy.

Sitting by an old gatepost, with only the railway line separating them from the walls of their rival church, Peggy realised that they had no plan for the next stage of the crime. They could count on the church being unlocked, but the work of the sewing wives would surely be locked away. The key to any office would be with the verger and the key to any cupboard would, probably, be lodged this moment beneath the pillow of the most truculent widow in the village.

Quietly, she offered to release the older woman from further involvement.

"I can't leave it to you, Peggy."

"Then call on the signal box keeper. People do, any hour of the day or night. He'll have a hot drink on his stove and a blanket to warm you up."

"No, Peg, no matter how many times you ask."

The stone walls of St Faith's, blue grey in the night time, gave the church a character unmatched by any other church in the diocese. The stone felt crumbly to touch. Weeds and moss grew in the mortar, home to robust creepy-crawlies that had delighted Victorian naturalists who believed they were unique to the neighbourhood. The two women in black approached from a corner of the graveyard where long grass grew and starved with the seasons, untouched by any gardener's shears. The headstones were sunken and disordered; some had broken and fallen forward into the dips of the ground, weighing heavy on the remnants of bodies buried in times beyond memory. Although Peggy believed in the quiet spirits of the dead, she had always dismissed talk of ghosts as the fancies of troubled minds, but, as she trod over the forgotten dead, she was ready for spectres to rise up from the uncultured ground; it was as if mortals were out of bounds on this blindside of the church.

The two women hid nervously against the church wall. Peggy saw a rook throw her head back and crow – but no sound issued from the open throat. When two rabbits stared from the cusp of their burrow, the women stood still and stared back. The creatures darted forward – but instead of racing in a pair, they crossed over each other's path. Peggy caught her breath, hoping that the school-ma'am hadn't noticed this omen of witchcraft. Miss Carstairs gripped Peggy's sleeve.

Footsteps approached, the sound of leather soles on cinders, but there were no chippings near and the footsteps were loud enough for any earthly figure to be seen and touched. Peggy stared into the cold mist above the ancient graves; it swirled and bowed, ready to give up the shape of something disturbed. She looked hard, so hard that her eyes smarted.

"But who?" Miss Carstairs whispered. The dead needed reasons to rise up.

Peggy remembered how she had nearly cricked an ankle as she stepped on one of the graves. At the time, she had steeled herself to make no noise about it – that had seemed enough – but that faltering step seemed more significant than ever now.

"They know what we're up to, Peg. One of the ancients has been tasked to guard their church against any burglary. One of the dead, Peggy. One of the dead."

Peggy's fingers went inside her vest to the miniature wooden crucifix that hung from her neck – a token, less than three quarters of an inch high and no broader than matchsticks – which she had fashioned from an offcut of her mother's headboard. She had promised to neither swear on it nor call on it to strengthen a prayer, but now she was ready to thrust it forward from her chest at any figure emerging from his grave.

The footsteps were so clear, so near, that there could be no doubt, but still the ghost hadn't formed himself. Miss Carstairs sensed that Peggy was seeking an explanation. "For Lord's sake, keep quiet, Peggy. Don't question, but show your faith in all things good."

Peggy raised her eyes to the skies and, at once, relaxed. Rain had soaked to the edge of the church eaves and dropped to a thatched ledge in great dollops that made the sound of soles on gravel.

"Miss Carstairs, you see?"

Miss Carstairs yelped and pulled down on Peggy's sleeve. "Aw, so horrible." She let go to cover her face with her hands. "I trod on it, Peg. Trod on the dead bird. Please, please toe it away. Oh Lord, I felt its little frail ribs ready to give in to the ball of my foot. I swear, I could feel its blood, just like a cushion beneath its skin." The old lady steadied her voice. "We're beyond the point of going back, but the Lord means to taunt us every step of the way."

Peggy decided on action in the place of dithering. "We've no ghosts to worry about," she said firmly, "only raindrops. And the bird was there long before we turned up. I'm tracing the church walls until I find a way in. Keep tag on my coat, Miss Carstairs."

The old schoolma'am said, "I never thought you'd be better than me at this."

Their narrow stone path crumbled away to soft soggy ground which was soon overtaken by brambles and shoots of wild bushes. In places they couldn't get near to the church walls and the old decrepit windows that might have let them in. By good luck some work had been done beneath the vestry window; the snags and snares had been cleared and someone had tried to build a hard-standing with broken bricks, but that idea had found insufficient favour. Miss

Carstairs stood on the little square and wobbled as Peggy leaned forward to test the window.

"It's rotten," she reported. "I can pull it open but the frame will come away in my hand. We'll never get it back again."

Miss Carstairs felt that little else could go wrong. "Go forward, Peggy. Get in and get out, and let's get home."

Working in the dark, Peggy prized open the right-hand window without difficulty, but the window wasn't hung on carpenters' hinges but relied on crude old fashioned joints, and the timber was so rotten that, as soon as it creaked open, it hung half-off its retainers. Peggy opened the second window, then pressed down on the ledge to lift herself into the room. But the ledge gave way. Worse, the top inch of stonework crumbled beneath her weight. And her boots were too loose to give her a purchase. "Oh, bloody," she said.

Miss Carstairs stooped down and took off the boots. Then she pressed two hands on Peggy's seat, counted to three and gave a timely push.

"Don't!" Peggy cried, too loudly. "I'll land on a table and everything will collapse."

"Be quiet, girl."

Peggy twisted and wheedled her way into the dark vestry and sat cross-legged on the floor as she tried to work out the best way forward. She crawled to the door; it was locked so she wouldn't be disturbed. Then she crept to the table, opened the drawer and checked for any bunches of keys; the drawer was empty.

She looked around here. "This room hasn't been used for years," she whispered.

Miss Carstairs' disorderly head appeared in the window-frame. "Try the box in the corner, dear. There's thread on the floor and wrappers from needle packets stuck on the table leg. I think this is the room for the sewing circle."

But Peggy didn't move. She thought she had heard someone enter the church and, like a canny creature in the hedgerow, she stayed still until she was sure that she was safe.

"All churches make noises in the night time," said Miss Carstairs.

"It's the water in their bones. No one's about, Peggy." She added to herself, "Who would be?"

The old sea chest was locked. Russian letters had been freshly painted in white on the tar covered lid. One side panel had been decorated like a scrap-screen. The key hung from a coat-hook on the vestry door. She knelt at the trunk, turned the key in the lock and tested the weight of the lid; she didn't want it to make a noise as she lifted.

"There's no one about," Miss Carstairs repeated. Peggy's fingers were red with cold, her feet were damp and her knees hurt from kneeling on the bare floorboards. She was sure that someone was walking up and down the nave.

Slowly, she raised the lid and lifted one of the tapestry cloths so that Miss Carstairs could see. The schoolma'am told her to waste no time, but Peggy paused to hold some examples of the needlework to the moonlight. Without doubt, everything she found was much superior to anything that her own church-kneelers could produce. If fair was fair, her village would lose the competition for a fourth year in a row.

"These are exquisite," she whispered.

She ran the back of a finger over the intricate stitch work, saying nothing.

Miss Carstairs broke the uneasy pause. "Peggy let's not do it. We've not done anything wrong before. We've still time to back down." The old schoolteacher was hearing all the advice she had given to young children. "Let's go home, Peg."

The village policeman's wife put her hand in the large pocket of the uniform coat and brought out a tiny envelope that Freddie Becker had passed to her, so proudly and so cagily, after tea. She opened the flap with her teeth but jerked her head back, not daring to sniff any of the bugs' eggs into her nose. She lifted the top half of the fabrics to one side and, following the young fellow's instructions, sprinkled a circle of eggs, lighter than the finest seeds, into the middle of a tapestry. She rubbed them in, then sprinkled a second circle over the same place and rubbed in that cohort. She spread some of the cloth over the treated layer, leaving a quarter of the load unpacked, and repeated the procedure.

"How does he know they're mites' eggs?" worried Miss Carstairs.

No one in the village knew little Freddie better than Peggy did. He trusted Peggy and would never want to let her down. Even if he had been tricked into swapping his sweets for something less than mites' eggs, he would surely have tested them and decided that they were something just as dreadful. But, more likely, he had no need to trade but had been culturing the bug-seeds in his woodland den for months. (After all, a young boy always has a need for things unspeakable.) "You naughty lad," Peggy smirked as she dug to the bottom of the pile and made two little nests of the eggs in the dusty corners of the box.

The evil had been done.

The lid squeaked at she lowered it; a pointless objection to being abused, but it needed to have its say.

"Peggy, don't let's do it. I can't think why I agreed to the idea. That's all it was, just an idea. Even if we don't get caught, they'll guess that we've been up to something. Peggy, it's wrong. I dare say that they won't be able to prove anything. They won't even accuse us, probably. But, Peggy, it's wrong. God, I feel dreadful."

But Miss Carstairs put her gloved hand over her mouth as Peggy dropped to the floor, then crept towards the door.

Clearly, now, she could hear footsteps treading up the stone nave, and they were footsteps which she recognised. Pinch. Why was Pinch patrolling St Faith's Church in the middle of the night? She held her breath as she heard him approach. Her eyes bulged as they watched the doorknob turn as he tested the lock.

He sensed that something was wrong; the policeman's wife could feel his curiosity. He knocked on the door, he tried the lock again, then grunted in resignation.

If she bolted for the window, the pair could be lost in the woods while Pinch was still hurrying out of the church and along the broken paths to the hidden side of the graveyard. Her flight would make plenty of noise, of course, but Pinch was an overweight and short of puff policeman. She chewed the knuckle of her little finger as she tried to decide what to do. She couldn't get away without alerting

Pinch, and alerting Pinch meant alerting the St Faith's Kneelers. They had come too far to spoil things. She made a silent signal to Miss Carstairs' face at the broken window; they had to see it through. Miss Carstairs nodded and her image sunk out of view. Peggy settled on the floor and pressed her ear to the wooden door panel.

Pinch pottered and plodded around the church in a fashion that Peggy recognised. This was the way that he moved around his home. He found the flagon of mild beer, which St Faith's vicar always left for those were passed through the church at night, and sat in the front pew with a quarter of a pint in a beaker. He brought his pipe from his pocket and the air was soon laced with the raw scent of his tobacco, a one-off mixture which the tobacconist called Bull's Dung.

A slight figure emerged from a dark corner. He walked with all collars up and his hands in a misshapen raincoat. He had a drawn look, with long lines on a lazy face. Here was a man who was used to being cold.

"You said we'd be alone." His voice was flat, as if he had nothing to offer the conversation. He had run out of promises and expected to be done to. "I can hear other people, Mr Pinch."

"Mice, rats and bats, and rooks that know no better. There's no one else about. The vicar has left some suppers in the pulpit."

The man moved away. The church and its mice made some more noises, and he returned with beer in a teacup and a wholesome slice of pie wrapped in muslin. "I'll go to prison for what I've done but I'll not stand for murdering my own sister."

"You stole the books."

"Only those as were pointed out to me. He said they should be delivered into safe hands."

"Who paid you?"

"I won't tell you, Mr Pinch. I was paid to take the books and take the blame. I'm wise enough to know that the country would fall to pieces if great personages were shown to be thieves."

"But Lakey was right to sack you?"

"I've no argument with that. I'm a well-read person, Mr Pinch, who loves his books. But working with letters and figures is a different matter. I know that I never pulled my weight in the office and when it came to letting men go, I knew that I'd be the one who was called up."

Joe Bidding dithered. He knew that he could finish the supper without filling his stomach but the last seven days, when he had lost his job and walked out of his home, had taught him how to manage his appetite. Sensibly, he should wrap the crust and some of the meat for the following day.

"Are you saying you stole the books from the office?" Pinch asked.

"Not those books, Mr Pinch. Those were already delivered into the safe hands. Do you think I'm clever enough to steal when your own chief constable is scurrying around the office?"

"What are you telling me?"

Pinch looked away as the man wrapped the remnants in the muslin and stuffed it untidily in the raincoat pocket. Joe Bidding was a man who would always be hungry. He said, "A great personage, whom I will not name, paid me to take books identified and pass them into his safe keeping. For that, I will go to prison. But I didn't steal from my employer and I had no part in murder."

Pinch chewed on his pipe stem, a habit that he derided in others. "Where were you when it was done?"

"You think I butchered my own sister?"

"I know you didn't but I need the whole picture, Joe."

"I had slept two nights in the open and I couldn't do a third. I'd heard that your verger was content to leave the outhouse open in the rector's garden if he knew someone was inside to look after things. So that's what I was doing, looking out for your verger."

"You didn't know your sister was in the village?"

Bidding shook his head. "I was told to look behind the post office. I wanted to keep off your main street so I went down the rough footpath."

"We call it the Waddie."

"But it wasn't the verger I saw. It was your rector speaking to the post-lady's brother at the back of their house. I kept out of sight, and hurried back to the vicarage. I hopped over the garden wall and hid in the bushes as the old chief came away from the front door and went through the gate. At that moment, the vicar appeared in the front street, but he was walking away from me. Towards your house, Mr Pinch. The chief followed him, as far as I know."

"As far as you know?"

"They were both walking down the hill but I didn't wait. I crept around to the back of the rectory. I was looking for the verger. What good would a rector be for me?"

"You must still have been in the village when the shout went up?"

"But I didn't know it was my sister, did I? The shout went up and I ran off. I was through your churchyard and into the woods before I stopped for breath."

Peggy - nibbling a fingernail, her ear pressed to the wooden door panel, her ankles aching because she was too nervous to move them - pleaded in her head, 'How long, Pinch? Ask him, how long?'

But it seemed that no more questions would be asked. Miss Carstairs was impatient, Peggy was tired and the village constable was content to take things no further. The church timbers creaked with damp; the church mice stayed still and silent, mother mice praying that their young wouldn't betray them. Black rooks waited long before answering one another's calls. The village houses were silent and dark; the church of St Faith's might have been in the middle of nowhere.

Pinch shuffled his feet. Bidding gave the dry cough of a sick man. 'Ask him,' Peggy begged.

"The vicar has left half a dozen food parcels in the pulpit," the policeman said. "He won't expect to find any there in the morning."

"But mothers of children will come at first light. I'll not take more before them. It does young 'uns no harm to go to school without breakfast but they're due a good tuck-in when they get home."

Oh, give me strength, Pinch. If you're not going to ask him how long, ask him about the woman with awkward shoulders.

Pinch stood up. Peggy pictured him shaking his clothes into shape and checking that no hair was sticking to the edge of his ears.

101

She expected him to say, 'Ah well, then,' but this time she was wrong. He went for more ale and, when he returned to his seat, he sorted out some change from his pocket. As he pressed it into Bidding's hand, he said, "I'll not see an honest man destitute," which, for all of Bidding's admissions, didn't seem out of place. "There's a job, Witney way. It's not much, just helping out in a greengrocers. But it's a start and there's lodging above the shop. I'll write and let them know that you're making your way. There's many who'd say that you should be proceeded against and if you stay in these parts, they'll get you. I know nothing of your 'great personage' but you and I know that he won't be called to account. You're a loyal fellow, Joe Bidding, but I say you've been badly used."

"You'll get into trouble?"

"I can talk fast when I need to."

The men were on their feet. Joe's eyes filled with tears as he shook the policeman's hand. "I owe you a good turn, sir. Bidding isn't a man who forgets and I'll repay before too long."

"Goodbye, Joe, and good luck."

No! Ask him!

Joe had walked the length of the nave before Pinch caught up with Peggy's thinking. "I need you to tell me, Joe. How long were you in the rectory garden before you heard the alarm?"

"A good time," he replied. "I know that the church clock chimed twice because I was marking the time. That would be quarter past and half past, so I was waiting for something short of twenty minutes. Eighteen minutes would be as accurate as any man could say."

Peggy jerked her head back from the vestry door. No. That didn't make sense. Bidding had to be fibbing. Otherwise, one … two … three other people had to be telling lies.

"Thank you, Joe. You'd make a good witness but I'll see that no one calls on you to give your evidence. Now, Godspeed."

Peggy was ready to shout out: arrest him, Pinch! Pinch! Don't let him go. But she knew that she couldn't give her game away.

They had stopped talking. Peggy heard Bidding walk away. Alone, Pinch had taken to walking around the church. He was reading inscriptions on the walls, all the time working through the implications of his witness's testimony. Peggy turned to see Miss Carstairs who, still and freezing in the square window frame, shook her head; they mustn't move until Pinch had finished his pottering and plodding.

Peggy gently eased her ankles into a more comfortable position. She leaned back to allow them better circulation, but misjudged her balance and toppled backwards.

Constable Pinch marched to the priest's cupboard and collected a bunch of keys on an old heavy ring. Peggy heard them clank as he approached and closed her eyes in dread. She saw Miss Carstairs raise a cautionary hand. Keep absolutely still, she meant. Pinch tried a key in the door lock. It didn't work so he turned to the second key on his bunch. This time, the mechanism turned, slowly and loudly.

In seconds, he would be in the room.

Peggy ran to the window. "Run, Miss Carstairs. Make the rendezvous before three!"

Kicking the table aside and tossing a three-legged stool in the air, she flung herself onto the ledge. "Save yourself!"

CHAPTER NINE
Suffer the Children

When Pinch stepped into the room, Peggy's arms were reaching for the ground outside while her legs paddled inside with no effect.

"Who's that?" the policeman demanded, his mouth full of something.

"Somebody else," she cried out, without thinking.

He took a step forward and went on chewing. "Peggy Pinch, is that you?"

"No."

"Peggy?" He wiped his mouth with the back of his hand, then licked.

"No, Pinch. I promise, Pinch, it isn't me."

She felt his hand grip the waistband of her trousers and he hauled her inside.

"Oh, Pinch, I'm so sorry," she rattled as she landed in a clump on the vestry floor. "I promise, I'm so sorry." She was already on the edge of tears. "Pinch, don't be cross with me. I can't stand it if you're angry again."

He made some suitably gruff noises but, in truth, he was too puzzled to be angry. He was determined not to mention that she was wearing his clothes and, worse, that she appeared to have lost a pair of his boots. With one hand, he brought his pipe from his left hand pocket while the other produced his tobacco pouch and matches.

Peggy opted for discretion. She knew that she was in trouble, again, but she wasn't sure how much trouble. He wasn't roaring at her, so she hoped she might get off lightly if she played a careful hand. She knew that her husband softened when she daydreamed, that he liked the look on her face when she tried to work things out and that he liked to correct her when she sucked her little finger. She tried all these things.

"Don't, for one moment, think that we won't go into these matters," he said, with a stern eye that made Peggy fidget on her feet.

She shook her head wildly.

"I suppose," he said, very carefully, "that you heard Joe Bidding's version."

She nodded her head, just as enthusiastically.

"Follow."

He led her to the nave where a key on his bunch unlocked a pokey room reserved for the churchwarden. Pinch lit low lamps while Peggy, saying that enough food could always be found in a church, without touching the parcels for the poor, if you knew where to look, went foraging. She came back with stale bread, pensioners' cheese, a pudding basin of Christmas fruits wrapped in cloth and a misshapen specimen which Pinch said was some sort of pear. She heated it over a flame and produced a welcome bread and cheese pudding. The married couple sat either side of a table meant for one. Pinch poured the wine. It occurred to her that they hadn't spoken properly since the goings-on in the police house kitchen.

"I've got to tell you something," she began.

"Peggy, I don't want to hear it."

"Really, I —-"

"Really, no," he insisted with his mouth full. "This pie is too delicious to spoil with true stories of your doings. Very good indeed, Mrs Pinch. How's home?"

"All the books are up to date."

"I knew you'd keep the family business running," he said with obvious satisfaction. "You have got my grey pipe with you?"

"I'm sorry, Pinch. I wasn't expecting to see you."

"No reason why you should." He paused, food still in his mouth, and sighed. "Brevitt is good enough and the vicar here keeps a good house, but I miss m'parlour pipes."

"Pinch, Verger Meggastones tricked his way into our kitchen last night."

"Wanting to spy on my experimentations, was he?" He started chewing again. Peggy reached for a basin's cloth which her husband made into a napkin and tucked into his open collar.

"I wouldn't have let him near your experimentations, though he didn't ask. Not your experimentations, no. Pinch, he was after being familiar with your wife."

"Scoundrel. I'm sure he came off worse."

"Pinch, I don't know what to do. I've locked him in our cell."

He spluttered his food as he laughed out loud. "My God, you did! Well done, girl."

"What if he tells?"

"Then he'll be laughed at. It will be none of your business when I bloody his nose. Let him explain that."

"You're not angry with me?"

"You know, I think I'm always angry with you. It's a matter of how much. Sometimes …"

"Yes?"

How could he say that he wished her mother was alive to offer advice? She had been the only soul able to manage their naughty Peggy.

She sighed. "I know. Sometimes, well sometimes, it seems that I've spent our whole marriage getting out of trouble. It's just as you say, Pinch. It's not a question of trouble, but how much trouble." She sighed and shook her head. "I promise I'll do better."

He asked, "Did Meggastones speak about the dead woman?" He poured himself some more of the vicar's second worst wine. "I think he knows more about the unfortunate Mrs Bidding."

"He thinks that the motive is the best clue to the murder and we should look for someone who knew her in their past."

Pinch looked up from his plate. "Does he? Interesting. Do you?"

"I don't see how that can be the key. It has to be somebody who was walking about the village at the time. They came and went from our garden, Pinch. I'm afraid none of my suspects are old enough to have sage knowledge of poor Ann Bidding. One thing I do know,

Joe Bidding was telling fibs. Either he or three others. Were you wise to let him go, dear?"

"A chap with a wing down, Mrs Pinch. I couldn't help myself but lend a hand. His important personage is Miss Carstairs, you think?"

"Pinch, how can you say that! I've known Clemency Carstairs all my life. She wouldn't steal!"

"I'm not so sure. She has something of the magpie and she's been acting strange these last weeks. This evening's mischief – just look – she took part readily enough."

"It —-"

"Yes, Mrs Pinch?"

"It was my idea," Peggy insisted. "I got it from the sheep."

His fork hovered above his dish. Sheep? How could any husband control a woman who took ideas from wandering sheep?

"If not Clemency Carstairs, then who?"

"The bishop, of course! The bishop, Pinch! I've checked the journals and ledgers and the books were stolen within a few days of a bishop's visit, and the dates marry Ethel's entry of money being received and spent by the church kneelers' circle."

Pinch weighed the evidence as a spoonful of bread and cheese pudding went around his mouth. "It doesn't have to be the bishop," he concluded. "It could just as likely be something else, making the most of the coincidence."

Peggy stayed quiet and watched her husband chew the last of his supper. The bishop's part in the affair had always been the starting point which, she thought, had led her towards the identity of the murderer. If that was wrong, if he wasn't the thief's sponsor, she needed to draw up a new list of suspects.

At a quarter to five, when Verger Meggastones was lighting the first oil lamp of the day and, in the Red Lion, the cellar man undressed for bed and, three doors up, old Mrs Frayle looked at her clock and conceded that she would find no sleep for the third night this week, Dorothy Becker gave up knocking on the police house door. She couldn't understand why Peggy, her one friend in the world, wasn't there to dissuade her but took it to be the clearest sign that God meant to put no obstacles in her path to heaven.

Wearing nothing but her nightdress, she wandered serenely - floating someone might have said - down the back footpath to the ford and walked, barefoot, along the banks of the brook. She watched its waters broaden and deepen. Her mind was settled. She didn't even feel cold. For two days in bed, she had searched to do something that would make amends for what she was. Now she knew that removing herself from the villagers was the one positive thing she could do to lift the troubles from their shoulders. Yes, they would be upset to find her gone, but that would be the very last pain she would cause. She felt no despair. She walked without hesitation. The stones didn't cut her feet, the hedges and brambles didn't snare her way.

As the shapes and sounds of the village became more distant and she walked towards the Horse Pool, which every child had been taught to avoid because of its whispering currents, she felt that she was coming home. Coming, not going.

She took off her nightdress and sat bare on the bank, just for a few moments, as she looked forward. It would be so comforting to look down on how things changed without her. Her mother growing old and, at last, having less work to do. She would be able to watch Freddie growing up, becoming a man with a role to fulfil and, no doubt, children of his own. Dorothy would be there, whenever he thought of her; she would be there in an everlasting way. She would always be his childhood sister and, over the years, the bad things that had happened to her would grow smaller.

She didn't fear the water; it would be easy, Jesus had promised her, like taking one step towards his outstretched hand.

She was up to her knees before she realised that she had slipped from the grass bank. The instant before she plunged, she saw the family of ducks on the other side. The mother was waiting for her. She had always known that it was God's little creatures that would care for her. Down. She was overtaken by exhilaration. Oh, how she looked forward to being free of this body. It didn't even feel hers, anymore. Spoiled, soiled and corrupted. Never before had she felt so dirty on the inside. Her bones and flesh and whatever they carried had been turned wicked. Good for nothing and something to be rid of.

Down. The water pulled and bathed her. It was cold, but it was a distant chill like reaching for something icy yet not touching it. She couldn't help but take one deep breath as her head went under – she knew that she wouldn't need any air but sucking in had been automatic. The water was making a mess of her hair but that didn't matter anymore. The current was spinning her around – one moment she was face down, the next she felt close to the surface. She needed to sink – and the moment she thought that, her legs were drawn down to the depths. She blew all her air out. Now, she needed to breathe the water in. One big go. She reached out her hand, seeking Jesus. Instead, she felt his arms cradling her shoulders. How clever that the first voice she heard was mother's. It was just like coming home.

"Silly!"

Ruby Becker was up to her knees, the skirts of her dress swirling in the currents. "You silly, silly, silly girl. Silly to think that I wouldn't be looking out for you."

Dorothy let herself be hugged closer. She was struggling to come back, to make sense of what was happening. Her limbs felt limp and heavy and, for the first time, her fingers and toes were chilled to the bone. Her teeth and jaws wanted to chatter but her mouth was so swollen. She wasn't sure that she could do whatever she was supposed to do.

Peggy Pinch was shouting, waving her arms as she ran downhill with two hundred yards to go.

Ruby trod two squelching steps towards the bank. She knew she couldn't climb out without throwing Dorothy ashore first but nothing could persuade her to part with her child. "Try, Dorothy. Keep trying for mother." Then, more desperately, "I tried for you, lass, now you try for me."

Footsore, short of breath and aching in every joint, Peggy forced herself through the last stretch of meadow, nature's extra push making light of the discomforts. Her feet hardly touched the bumpy ground and she never questioned her balance. She seemed to fly until, at last, she dropped to her knees and slid to the water's edge with both arms outstretched. "Give her to me, Rube."

The naked child was white, cold and limp.

"She's gone, Peggy," wept her mother as she climbed ashore.

"We'll not give up on her. Strip yourself to the waist, Ruby, so she can feel your flesh."

Ruby Becker hesitated.

"Oh, God, Ruby. I know no more than you, but it seems a mother's thing to do. Try it."

The woman ripped open her bodice and vest until she was showing all she'd got from her neck to the pit of her belly. Peggy passed the child to her, face first. But Ruby turned her and held her back to her skin. She bent forward. There was something, just a flicker, but it sounded more like life expiring than sparking up.

"Her soul has left us, Peg. I've never known her weigh so little."

"Keep trying. Tell the Almighty that you won't give her up."

Ruby squeezed beneath the child's ribs and bent forward. Peggy began, "Blessed are the children for they ..." and the duck, leaving her brood in the shelter of the waterweeds, flapped herself onto the bank. Desperate to try anything, no matter how obscure, Peggy picked up the bird and pressed her to the child's lap. The docile duck made no sound but settled herself deeply and stretched her neck up to Dorothy's throat. Rain had fallen in heavy isolated drops from a cloudless sky and trickled down her forehead.

Ruby lost hope. She wanted to lay her child peacefully on the grass. "Don't bother her," she whispered. "We must let her go, please."

But Peggy pushed her neighbour forward again. "Tell the Almighty," she repeated. "Say it. Say you won't give her up." This time, Dorothy emitted a deep growl, like a cow's belch, and threw up the water from her lungs. She tried to breath in, but couldn't. The duck started to peck rapidly at the pale swollen mouth. Harshly, Peggy grabbed the child's head, put fingers down her throat and pressed. She twisted her fingers, made a hook of them, she shook and waggled them. At last, Dorothy vomited debris and drew in fresh cold air.

Then, weirdly, the bird stretched her wings, drew back her shoulders and flew forward, as if she were life awakening.

The three figures were crying and exhausted. Ruby lay on her back, her daughter nestled at her side, her fingers reaching for her mother's face, her own face still wanting to draw comfort from her mother's nakedness. Perhaps Peggy did the most crying. She flopped back, rolled full circle and wept in a way that tried to get rid of everything that had happened.

Dorothy was the first to wake. When Peggy opened her eyes, the girl had dressed and was sitting cross-legged, contentedly making a chain from blades of grass. The day was coming to life, the sound of tractors and carts punctuating the air. Smoke across the hedges, far off, showed the progress of an early morning train. Milk churns were being clanked at gates and Mrs Duck was fifty yards downstream.

"You've got no shoes," Dorothy observed.

"I've been up to no good again," winked Peggy. "Shall we wake up mother? We need to get her to bed so that she can sleep properly."

Dorothy nodded, ready to be grown-up again. "She needs to sleep well."

As Driver David waited at the war memorial for passengers, just two days after the murder, he watched the news of Dorothy's rescue reach through the village. Gary Willowby was running errands between the vicarage kitchen, the Red Lon and the fishmonger's wagon on the church green. Postmistress Mary left Baby Michael in charge of the shop and joined Miss Carstairs and Mrs Porter in the middle of the road. They were arranging a roster of the most sensible and wise wives to support the troubled household. (They knew that laundry and the larder were the first household chores to be neglected. Even the most distracted mother would find time to wash floors; it was an exercise that got rid of so much worry.)

The doctor with his black medicine bag called at the cottage without a summons, followed a few minutes later by the vicar. He was carrying his parson's pocketbook close to his chest as if it were

111

a prayer book. The senior wives of the village wouldn't call until the vicar had gone.

Mrs Porter poked her head through the passenger door of the bus without mounting the step. "You won't be leaving for a while, will you?" Queen O'Scots climbed aboard and settled herself against the warmth of the engine housing. "You've got a magazine to read," Mrs Porter observed, nodding to the hobby magazine resting on David's steering wheel.

When Peggy made a similar enquiry a few minutes later, she caught him looking at some well-thumbed leaves of Bits of Fun folded into the pages of the wireless monthly. "I need to be in town before lunchtime but I must speak with the vicar first. You'll allow me twenty minutes, dear David?"

I'm happy to wait for an hour if it yields one passenger, he thought.

She brought him up to date with news of the little girl. "She's talking to her mother at last." Soon she would be accepting treats – hot drinks and buttered muffins – with a readiness that suggested childish indulgence rather than grudging acceptance of sweeteners to go with her medicine. Her brother was playing contentedly on the back step and the house, which had been shut up yesterday, would soon be taking calls from the neighbours. People next door were always the last in the pecking order; they stayed courteously away until the do-gooders had completed their business and mother and daughter were unbothered and ready to accept some company without a need to answer questions. The vicar's wife wouldn't call until the following day.

But the village's sigh of relief - and that was how it felt for those two hours in the middle of the morning – had a taste of the quiet before a storm. Young Dorothy Becker had come safely through her crisis, thank God, but people knew that one of their number would be accused of murder before long.

There was tetchiness is Miss Moorcroft's complaint to the fishmonger and Postmistress Mary felt uneasy about being absent from the post office for so long. Baby Michael's collie - which should run free now that Pinch, his main tormenter, was gone from the village – kept out of the way. The mother duck kept her brood close instead of leading them around the lanes and twitchels in their familiar train.

Old Mrs Frayle was sitting on her front porch with a blanket over her knees rather than watching proceedings from her parlour window. And when, at last, Gary Willowby found himself at a loose end, it was to the old maid that he went. "So you feel it too," she commented, knowing that the lad wouldn't understand. (She might have been talking to a pet.) He didn't answer but sat quietly on her step. He had never before had anything to do with Mrs Frayle.

Peggy sat on the war memorial bench and tried to place where everyone had been at the time of the murder. Surprisingly few couldn't be fitted into the jigsaw. Then, once the players were in place, she went carefully through the sequence of events. The answer had always been the same. Only one person could have killed Ann Bidding – but how could she prove it?

At a quarter to eleven, she went to the post office and pretended to be absorbed by the display shelf until the vicar emerged from the Beckers' cottage. He stood at the verge, adjusted his hat and the lapels of his well-bedded sports-jacket, then turned towards the vicarage.

Peggy caught him in the middle of the road. "Shortly before the body was found, you were talking to a tramp on the church green."

The vicar was sure that this wasn't the day for Peggy Pinch's investigations. Yes, two days ago, he had reminded her that her neighbours would need her, but they didn't need her like this. He sighed and patted his pockets. "That poor family are bearing up well, Mrs Pinch. They have made a bed for Dorothy in the parlour and her mother is sitting with her. I'm sure their household can't allow the shop in their back garden to be closed for another day. I was hoping that someone might be able to spare a couple of hours. Mrs Porter, do you think?"

"Vicar, the tramp. He wasn't the tramp that everyone knows around here. I think it was Mr Bidding."

113

The vicar decided to allow this one question, but no more. "He has lost his job and his home, Mrs Pinch. He's a soul struggling to put things right."

"Did he tell you about the books?"

"Books? He told me that he had taken the blame for the loss of one book from his employer's office. Were there others?"

"Did he tell you whose fault it was?"

"On the contrary. He emphasised that the blame was his alone. He weakened to a moment's temptation."

"What happened next, vicar?"

"Mrs Pinch, these investigations are best left to the police. Your toing and froing hardly endears you to your neighbours."

Baby Michael was already, temporarily, at the back of the bus. He knew that Peggy wanted to travel to town and he was waiting to see what seat she took.

"Reverend Fripps, I have never been popular. I have a husband and a home that I don't deserve and I fall into the trap of being right in what I say. Some women will love to tell you stories about me, while others are content to smirk and smarm when I'm in trouble, yet again. Most of the trouble, like most of the stories, I bring on myself. But a corpse was found in my bicycle shed – someone brought hideous savagery into my home – and many people saw my husband with a knife in his hand with blood dripping. Mind your own business, Peggy Pinch, they say. And never has that phrase been truer. No one owns this murder more than I do."

As red cheeked Mrs Porter grasped the handle bar at the bus door, she said, loud enough for Peggy to hear, "That woman has plenty to say to our vicar."

Jasmine Moorcroft, pressed up behind her, joined in. "She should've been there when the child knocked on her door. Where was she at four in the morning?"

Peggy wasn't ready with an answer. Without thinking, she barked, "I was seeing Pinch!" But she knew that her response would prompt more questions. The two women made a fuss of climbing aboard, then installed themselves on the front seat, meant for four.

"Righteous anger," the vicar observed. "I'll tell you. After our conversation, Bidding walked down Wretched Lane and into the fields. I watched for a minute or two." He recommenced his walk. "A vicar in Cardiff has promised to visit Janet McPherson this morning. He knows her mother well. It seems that we must expect sad news."

"Vicar, I do need to know where you went next."

Postmistress Mary came striding across the road, drying her hands on a tea cloth and forgetting that she was out of doors in carpet slippers. "You get off that bus now Michael! Clean the back store, I said, and you've not touched it." Her brother was out of his seat and at the door to meet her. "We're days behind," she shouted. "We've more to do than I've time to think about, d'you hear?" She followed him back to the post office, ready to slap the back of his head if he slowed down but he kept two paces ahead of her. Freddie Becker, leaning over his front gate, watched and sniggered.

Driver David tucked his magazines beneath the loose cushion on his seat and, after four or five attempts, got the engine going. He gave two long blasts on the horn to announce that he was ready to leave.

"They are waiting for you, Mrs Pinch," said the vicar.

"Vicar, please. Where did you go after speaking with Bidding?"

"There are occasions when a parson's progress through the day is better kept to himself. Just as your troubles indoors do not always benefit from daylight. Good day, Mrs Pinch."

CHAPTER TEN
Town Affairs

Fifty minutes late but without a grumble from the three passengers, the bone-shaking bus pulled away from the grass verge of the war memorial and trundled down the village lane. It slowed at the ford, then spluttered up the hill but no one doubted that the bus would keep going or that Porter and Moorcroft would run out of steam.

"Just how much does that man do for our church?"

"One can never tell, Mrs Porter."

"My point, dear Jasmine. Exactly my point."

Their two fat figures joggled in unison as the bus swayed and bumped along. Peggy, two rows back, glared at them. She hoped that her stare might burn the backs of their necks.

"He'd have us believe that he works in mysterious ways."

"Mysterious ways, Jasmine? Too much of me thinks that he's up to no good. I mean, who calls him to account for his day?"

Peggy kept quiet. One day soon would present an opportunity for her to make a snide remark about their criticism of the vicar. A life-time's watching and listening had shown her that forbearance always pays profit. Forbearance, Peggy Pinch; something you'd do well to practise.

The bus progressed along 'the edge', past the line of trees and the Wishing Pool, the stump of the old windmill and the crossroads where Peggy had been surrounded by sheep the day before. Gradually, they drew close to the course of the railway line and they caught their first glimpse of the market town.

"Have you seen him this morning?" Mrs Porter asked. "Of course, you haven't."

"Of course not," her dear Jasmine agreed.

"He'd be different with a wife."

Oh, Good Lord! They weren't talking about the vicar. They were talking about Verger Meggastones. Good Lord, thought Peggy. My Lord, he's still locked in the cell!

Having helped the Becker girl home, Peggy had returned to the police house. She had changed into her own clothes. She had sat on the back step with a cigarette and a pot of tea. She had washed up in the kitchen. She had walked past the cell window on her way to the garden toilet. But she had forgotten all about her prisoner. He hadn't shouted to her. No yelling or banging and kicking on the door. Oh Good Lord, what if he were dead?

She felt her hands sweat. A dozen ideas ran through her head, but none of them made sense. Be steady, she told herself. She had already planned to visit the police station. From there, she would telephone Miss Carstairs and ask her to provoke some response from the locked dungeon. Miss Carstairs would know what to do, whatever she found.

It didn't feel like a good plan but what else could she do? How could she ask Porter, Moorcroft or Driver David for help without explaining the unexplainable? The bus rolled onto the forecourt of the motor engineers and everyone got to their feet. After some discussion (Peggy took in little of it), David agreed to pick them up from the edge of the market square at four o'clock. He would be in the White Horse if they needed to leave early or stay late. As Peggy climbed down, she muttered aloud, "Clemency Carstairs will know what to do." Mrs Porter, gathering her bags on the pavement and straightening her coat and frock about her, caught the worried words and looked unnecessarily smug as she savoured Peggy's discomfort.

It was market day and the town square heaved with wagons, livestock and farmers. The men chewed on pipe stems or carried mugs of warm beer. Many seemed to be doing nothing at all. They propped themselves against the old iron railings of the temporary pens. Some might have been saving their places but others were there

117

because, well, everybody had to be somewhere. The smell and muck had drawn together man and animal-kind who were happiest when they were dirty. Like old sweats soaking in dirty baths, they had resolved to say little and, when they needed to speak, they managed to say it in no more than five words at a time. The main sale of the day was over. The auctioneer had mounted the rostrum, ready to manage a subsidiary sale but he couldn't begin until he had settled some confusion with his clerk. Peggy kept to the edge of the circus; she needed to get to the police station and had no other business in town. When she caught a conversation, it was grunts and nods and broken phrases that ought to have been wise but made no sense. She recognised Thurrock's lead stockman, marking squiggles on folded notepaper as he went from pen to pen. Children were learning the ropes, making play of their work. But it was the old men –bent and crooked with faces twisted by the years – who held the permissions. Even farmers in their forties and fifties had to look to the master generation before deciding their best bids.

At the market cross, the duty patrol sergeant was trying to avoid arresting a drunken woman who had punched a cowman's face. "He took me for a have-as-you-may," she argued. "What would you want me to do? I had to learn him his lesson afore he went too far."

That's just how it was, thought Peggy, her mind turning over what might be found in the police house cell.

"Self defence, ser'nt. Who's on the bench as'd say it were otherwise?"

"Lock her up, corporal!" someone shouted from the crowd.

The woman turned her back on the policeman and went in search of the cat-caller, leaving the bruised farmer to be collected by his fellows.

Peggy hurried across the road, strewn with vegetable leaves and squashed fruit from the barrows lined along the opposite kerb. Two women were shelling peas on a pub doorstep and a porter, with two crates on his head, kept a straight back as he avoided other walkers.

The police sergeant shouted a welcome but Peggy couldn't wait. She needed to get to a telephone and ask Miss Carstairs to peer through the cell window. She turned away from the market and marched past the established shop fronts, many of them Georgian. Pinch's favourite tobacconist, the stationer, wine-seller, two haberdashers and the shop called Parlourphones with its window display of magical music making machines.

Suddenly Moorcroft and Porter were at her either shoulder. "Walk on, Peggy Pinch," said Porter. She had started her day with fortified wine and now gin was on her breath. "Make out the three of us are heading for the Cat and Copper Kettle tea shop."

"I'm going to police headquarters," Peggy said without slackening.

Moorcroft got close to her ear. "I can smell a woman who's carrying," she said nastily. "I can sniff it, fifty yards away."

"Who d' you think you are, Jasmine Moorcroft? If I was in any condition – which I am not – it was be business for my husband and me."

"Some say it would be no business of Pinch."

"How dare you!" spat Peggy

But Moorcroft wouldn't concede. "There's many believe you've taken a lover, Peggy Pinch."

Peggy stopped, caught hold of the woman's coat sleeve and turned her round. "You poisonous hag! You wouldn't say these things if we were home in our village. What are you about?"

"People talk," smirked Moorcroft.

"I don't have to listen to lies!"

"You'd do well to take notice, you footloose young tartar," the Porter woman scowled.

"Take notice, Peggy Pinch," they chanted together. They squeezed Peggy from the gap between them and ambled off, Porter relying on the other to keep her straight.

Peggy was dazed. She stood at the street corner, stepping back and forward as people pushed past her. She didn't see the heads that turned to look and the faces that approached, wondering if they should speak.

The police sergeant saw that she was lost and started to make towards her, but Peggy knew that he would be no refuge; he'd ask questions, he'd want to know what she was doing in town. And what could she say when he asked if the women had been bothering her?

Could a woman be accused of anything worse than taking a man? The sergeant was waving to her now and quickening his pace as he mounted the pavement.

Peggy turned away, stumbling a little as she hurried off. She needed some tea and, avoiding the Cat and Copper Kettle, she turned down a side alley to the rough and ready stop where farmers in boots and working women in aprons and rolled up sleeves parked themselves between proceedings. It was a noisy place with a dirty wet floor and five or six people to each table. The walls were decorated with colourful advertisements for beers which the café wasn't licensed to sell.

Peggy grabbed a seat in a corner, with no table, and when the woman at the counter shouted "Tea, my duck? With a heaped spoonful?" Peggy nodded and mumbled, though no one could hear.

"That's one sugar, is it, my love?"

She nodded again.

The cup was passed from hand to hand across the room. Content to be out of place, she sat against the wall. The tea was thick with milk, spoilt with sugar and stewed to a brown tan. A dog licked a plate clean at her feet, her neighbour kept a handkerchief in his hand to wipe phlegm from the side of his mouth and the air was thick with smoke from the harshest tobaccos.

From a table, diagonally opposite and the centre of attention from those around it, a scruff stood up and pushed chairs aside as he strode across the room. "What's a copper's woman doing with us?" he challenged. He had curly blonde hair that hadn't been combed and wire rimmed spectacles that looked as if they belonged to somebody else. His cheap suit was misshapen with stretched pockets and curled lapels. He tapped Peggy's neighbour on the shoulder. The man grumbled and fidgeted but didn't resist being displaced.

"You've got to be here because of the murder." He produced a dog-eared business card from his top pocket, as he sat down. "I'm Harry Hawk from the Weekly Advertiser."

A bookie's runner was handing out slips behind the door and the proprietor was taking money for something under the counter. Peggy noticed a mirror standing on the shelf behind her which gave anyone in the back room a good view of what was going on in the café.

"Please, Mr Hawk. I've nothing to tell you."

"Then what you doing here?" he persisted. "Not at all your sort of place, mixing with the likes of us." He leaned his head back and stretched his legs where there was no room. "Someone important needs protecting, that's what they're saying. Pinch has been banished and the detectives have been called off until the investigation cools down. What can you tell me?"

A child appeared from nowhere and started to sweep dog-ends from the floor. He wore no underwear beneath his patched trousers and one sandal was slightly odd to the other. He kept his face down as he came near Peggy; he wasn't allowed to let people talk to him.

A young man wanted to dispute the bookie's deal but too many others knew that matters should be kept quiet. Hawk relaxed, his head back against the wall, and watched it all go on. Peggy sensed the contentment of a man whose day was his own. Was he really employed by the paper or just a lucky man who was in with it? This unsavoury man from the Advertiser, Peggy decided, was a fixer.

"I don't know what you're talking about," she said.

"Oh, but I think you do. I think you know very well. Whose face are you saving, Mrs Pinch?"

"I've told you. I know nothing about it. Please, I've had a bit of a shock."

"Do you know what I think? I think someone should set a firework in their britches. Are you the lady to do that?"

Peggy picked up her handbag and gathered her coat as she got to her feet. "Really, I need to be going." She didn't look back but pushed her way through the tables and chairs. Straightaway, the child went to her place, hoping for something better than the ordinary litter.

The street was too busy for her. Market day was over for most of the farmers and dealers and the town was alive with the racket of loading and dismantling. Animals were being driven down the street. Wagons with fowl crates were wobbling as they navigated the cobbles and kerbstones. Instructions were called from every quarter.

Prices and weights were chalked – sometimes scratched – on any spare patch of wall. Some families would be here until six, hoping to snatch a mean living from the waste and near waste. Market scavengers, Pinch called them. Some of these strugglers brought their barrows to the village but their stock was never good enough for Ruby Becker to take into her back garden shop. One had been standing his handcart on the church green since Peggy's childhood. Of course, he looked no older than he had been twenty years ago.

Peggy wanted nothing to do with the commotion. Her world was on the edge of falling apart. She knew who had committed the murder but that was a long way from bringing him to justice. The killer couldn't consider his job well done until he had finished off a second victim. Worse, as Dorothy regained her senses she became more of a threat to him. If Peggy couldn't convince the chief constable to make an arrest today, the murderer might realise that she was on his trail and be pushed into action.

If Peggy failed, she would be left with more dead bodies, a husband at the end of his tether, a thirsty verger locked in her police cell, and neighbours who thought she was a pregnant adulteress.

"Quick march, Peggy Pinch," she said to herself. Police headquarters was at the bottom of town, a long way from the sounds of the market and the busy shops.

A lifetime of tell-tales had taught her that rumours always start with a nugget of truth. So, what had Peggy done that nosey parkers might have misinterpreted? Yesterday, she had risen early so that she could waylay Mr Becker as he cycled to work. Last night, she had invited Meggastones into her home after dark and prying eyes would have detected that he had stayed all night. Then, she had followed Poacher Baines into the woods. Baby Michael had a soft spot for her, but that had been going on since their childhoods and Peggy had always been careful not to encourage him; as far as she could remember, she had never been seen alone with him.

She stepped off the kerb, wanting to cross, but stepped on again when she saw Hawk of the Advertiser waiting on an opposite corner. Somehow, he had got ahead of her. (Had she mentioned that she was heading for the police station?) His ferret face was laughing at her and his hands shuffled excitedly in their pockets. She looked over her shoulder, hoping that the policeman might still be there, in case the reporter bothered her. Another twenty yards and Porter, coming out of a hat shop, almost tumbled into her. At first each woman wanted to ignore the other. Then Porter broke the silence: "Have you seen Moorcroft? Left her in the bakery with clear instructions. Meet me at the clock tower before quarter past. Blast the woman if she can't keep to time."

Peggy mumbled and twisted her hands.

"Take note, Pinch. Hear what's said to you." And the woman was off again, the heaviness of her footsteps trying to disguise their uncertainty. She must carry her drink in a flask, Peggy thought.

The stout figure stood still in the middle of the road and raised an arm. "Take note, Peggy Pinch" she called out, then turned in a circle to damn the complaining traffic.

Surely, Miss Carstairs would have tipped off Peggy if folk were talking. And why hadn't the vicar hinted that she should be more careful? They had been talking alone on the street just minutes before she climbed aboard the bus. Oh Lord, no; surely, no one could think that she knew the village vicar too well.

But perhaps no particular gentleman was at the heart of the rumour. Perhaps she had been seen waiting too long at a corner of a village lane, or looking expectantly up and down from her garden gate, or taking on a sheepish look when the wrong thing had been said. And then, what if Moorcroft's sixth sense was correct and Peggy was already carrying without knowing it? But how?

Now look, she sighed in her head. This is all nonsense. Peggy had done nothing that merited being talked about. The story was an out and out fib. But who would want to start the tittle-tattle? Both Moorcroft and Porter were malicious enough to put it about but both were too careful to make it up. Peggy could think of many people who would enjoy hearing her reputation rubbished, but the liar needed a stronger reason beyond simple titillation. Which of her neighbours had something to gain from starting the rumour?

As Peggy crossed a fork in the road and, at last, the curious building that was Police Headquarters came into view, she realised that the murderer was the man most likely. She was almost running now. Her footsteps, her quick breathing and the short swing of her arms produced a rhythm that allowed no time for further pondering. She had business to do, and that business was the prompt arrest of the bicycle shed killer.

CHAPTER ELEVEN
Headquarters

With a rattle and clunk, Sergeant Robbo's face appeared at the ticket office window. "What can I do for you, Mrs Pinch? We have no trains."

When the Barton and Waters Railway collapsed before any train had run and the constabulary acquired the redundant terminus, the county's lieutenant, Colonel E. W. Palmerstone, supported the purchase on condition that the building retained its railway character. Police Headquarters was soon nicknamed Palmerstone's Folly but it was unfair to give him all the credit; every policeman reinforced the building's peculiar past. They spoke of the ticket office, booking hall and waiting rooms. The suite of cells was called 'goods inwards', work rosters were timetables and the bobbies paraded before duty on platform one. The colour scheme had provoked some discussion because the B. and W. hadn't travelled far enough to design a corporate identity; in the end, the headquarters were painted in the lord lieutenant's regimental colours, providing an obvious clue of where the paint had come from.

"I need to see the chief constable urgently."

"Ooh, I wouldn't know about that." Robbo scratched his head, buttered his lips, then brought down the shutter. Seconds later, his face reappeared. "The chief constable, you say?"

"Please, tell him I must."

Behind the closed shutter, he made a phone call in his thick local accent. Then Peggy heard retreating footsteps as he left the ticket office.

Peggy walked around, admiring the seaside prints on the walls, then sat down on the cold wooden bench. A woman came in, complaining to Peggy about the traffic in the Market Square but she left before Robbo opened his shutter. A young man wanted to know if a gentleman's umbrella had been handed in and a farmer announced that he was going to shoot his neighbour's dog and Robbo had better arrest him now. "I know how you feel about it, Dec Robinson."

A second sergeant came to the booking hall. This one had a crown above his three stripes. He sat beside Peggy. "What's this about, Peg? Has Pinch been up to no good?"

"I want to see the chief constable. He knows what it's about."

"We're a family here, you see. I can always have a word with brother Pinch if he needs putting right."

"It's nothing to do with my husband. It's to do with the chief constable."

"Ah, then it would be about Khartoum or the Valley of the Six Hundred. Rourke's Drift, no doubt."

"I want him to lead an expedition."

"By God, you do!" laughed the sergeant. "Chiefie will love you for it. Robbo! Saddle the white horse. Our leader leads from the front."

Raucous laughter echoed from the closed ticket office.

"Mrs P, I will let the inspector know just as soon as he's finished reading his morning newspapers. You'll make do with an inspector? For the time being? As a start, maybe?"

"Sergeant, I will make do with no one. Please tell your chief constable, I am here."

"That's certainly what I shall tell our inspector, Mrs P," he said as he withdrew.

Next, they tried the cleaner. She came with two teas (railway crests on the cups) and took her place on the bench. She had lost three front teeth and the backs of her hands were bruised. A rude woman, Peggy labelled her from the start. "Always difficult, dear. A woman hardly knows what to do when her man gets handy. You wouldn't believe the stories I've heard in this booking hall. Not that I'm one to mention names. Drink up your tea, my love."

126

Peggy observed, "It seems that this police station knows more than it ought about what passes between me and my husband. I've nothing to complain about."

"There's a good girlie. Let me tell you what old Mr Pinch really likes." She leant forward, her breath heavily scented with violets. "A heavenly bust. That's what tickles your husband."

No woman with manners would have put a stranger on the spot with such vulgarity.

The revelation was so inappropriate that Peggy didn't know how to answer. You're good for nothing but mopping floors, she wanted to say.

"You remember when he was in trouble, two years ago? They made him wait in the porter's cabin for more than an hour before calling him in for a right telling off."

Peggy didn't know what she was talking about. Pinch had mentioned no inquiry or reprimand.

"Afterwards, it falls to me - doesn't it? - to clean up the room and I find - don't I? - old Pinch's drawings of women in corsets. Half a dozen, all intricately done, with corsets drawn so tight as to make celestial busts on each woman. I'll let you have them, if you like. As soon as I picked them up, I thought these are too good to throw away."

"I want to see the chief constable."

The cleaner laid a crooked hand on Peggy's arm. "And don't you settle for anything less, dearie." She collected the cups and saucers and, repeating her last advice, walked backwards through the door.

The farmer returned, steam coming out of his ears. He stood in the middle of the booking hall, feet apart, hands waving above his shoulders. "They think they can ignore me!" he roared at Peggy. "That bleddy Robbo doesn't know what I've gone through!"

Peggy held out a hand. "Please, sit down. Tell me what the dog's done."

"I know what I'll do." He yelled, "Are you listening bleddy Robbo? I'll get Hawk from the Advertiser and he'll blow up your police station and everyone in it!"

"No. Now, you don't mean that."

But the farmer had already departed.

Sergeant Robbo lolloped into the hall. "What was that man threatening? Look, I've had enough of that scoundrel. I'll lock him up for threatening outrage and mayhem. God preserve me if I don't." He ran to the entrance doors.

"I must see the chief constable."

The senior sergeant appeared. "We can't have you swearing before Mrs Pinch, Robbo. Have you let that man go?"

Red-faced and furious, Robbo blustered, "He's promising outrage!" He was trapped between the double doors that wanted to close.

"Then we'll preserve the peace, Sergeant Robinson. That is our job."

The inspector, a bean-pole of a man with feet too large for his legs, marched in and strutted around with his cane. "Lord above, it's the Pinch-wife." He went to the entrance. Robbo had extricated himself and was searching the little garden. "Sergeant! You can't park Mrs Pinch here like some left luggage"

"I'm here to see the chief constable."

"Don't talk nonsense," barked the inspector. He was more concerned about Sergeant Robinson's lack lustre performance.

Peggy stood up, ready to press her case, but she felt the cleaner tugging at her coat sleeve.

"You come with me, dearie. Leave the men to their barracking and barging. Don't give us a minute's peace, those two. Always falling out over something, they are."

Peggy was taken on a winding trek through the passageways and staircases of the converted railway station. Locked travelling trunks and bulging mailbags had been posted in the way.

"It's my job to keep the clocks right."

"A task that must take some time," Peggy remarked quietly, for clocks seemed to hang on every wall.

"First thing in the morning and last thing at night. Forty-two in all."

Then, at one corner, Peggy was brought up by an oversized manikin dressed in an immaculate uniform with all accoutrements.

She was irritated by the smutty woman's natter about heavenly busts, good strong busts, prominent busts and busts the chaps would only find in Paris. "Our lads weren't the same when they came back from the war. Learned too much, if you ask me. Too much that should have been left in France." French busts, she meant. It was a conversation that Peggy wouldn't have tolerated from her closest friend, yet she was supposed to endure it without embarrassment from a woman who was certainly something less than a policeman's wife.

"Now don't you go thinking badly of Mr Pinch just because he draws pictures of soldier-like, thrusting busts. A man could daydream of much worse, you know."

The cleaner didn't reveal the offending doodles until she was sitting with Peggy in armchairs in an underground alcove. This was her secret place where the police force had no cause to nose. She had brightened the corner with two vases of flowers and a picture stolen from some other wall. Through the day, she kept a kettle close to boiling over a single gas flame. She stored her own cutlery in a wooden box designed to hold boot polish and brushes.

"The chief will see you when he's done with his ales," she said and brought a brown paper packet from her apron pocket. "Here, you look through these while I listen to your stories of the murder,"

The pen and ink drawings were no worse than Driver David might have found in his pages of Bits of Fun, and Peggy had already promised herself not to be shocked by fancies which her husband had never intended to share with her. Strangely, she was reassured to find that her husband's notion of ladies underwear was out of his head. No woman could ever dress like this in real life. But, oh, why had he been so foolish to let them fall into the wrong hands?

"I didn't know," she said.

"Like I say, dear, you give our Mr Pinch a good honest bust and you'll have no more trouble from him."

"I mean, I didn't know that he could draw." And then: "He's giving me no trouble. My husband is a good man. He has much to put up with."

"I'm sure, my dear, but you do as I say."

"These are so detailed. The laces and button holes, I mean, and even the embroidery. Really, he has a talent for it."

Then the woman returned to the sort of busts she preferred. A good bust, she said, reminded her of a good bull.

Peggy hoped that she wouldn't be kept here for a cup of tea with this vulgar woman. She didn't like women in towns, she decided. "I shall keep these," she said, making sure that the loose pages were safely tucked away.

"You must, dear. Now, they're saying as the woman's head was cut clean off."

"That's nonsense. She was stabbed in the chest."

"And her bodice was ripped open so that her insides were on show." The woman wiped a bubble from her lip.

"Is that what they say? Policemen shouldn't make up such stories."

Peggy didn't want to be questioned. She stood up but, before she could ask the way to the chief constable's office, the woman said, "I've heard the detectives say that it were the children, likely as not. They put their heads together and —-"

Peggy clenched her fingers, her head went forward. "Who's saying that? That's horrid and cruel. You're a wicked woman. You're rude and coarse. I've never met an old baggage like you!"

"Dearie, I was only saying. I've been trying to help you. We all know as how Mr Pinch takes a leather to your arse."

Without thinking, Peggy threw a slap at the woman's face, but the witch caught her wrist and tossed it aside.

"God, how I hate that word!"

It had spilled through the woman's yellow decayed teeth like overcooked gruel —- foul, sticky and smelling.

"That's not true!" Peggy shouted.

"I showed you those pictures out of kindness, dear," she said, with the pecking nose of a do-gooder betrayed, "never meaning to cause trouble. 'Though I see as you've got little of an honourable bust to win him over."

"Stop it! Stop your filthy, filthy talk. You live down here, like living in the drains. That's where you get your poison from. Your mouth's no better than a sewer. I hate you!"

130

She ran over stone floors and wooden floors and up an iron staircase towards welcome daylight shining through a window. People were laughing at one end of the building and laughing at another. The voices bounced in her head, turning into the hideous cackle of the old hag. She wanted to shut it out; she ran with her hands over her ears so that she wouldn't hear if she screamed.

Every soul in the police force thought they knew what happens in her police house kitchen. What they didn't know, they embellish from their imaginations so that the tales grew more titillating with each telling. More titillating for them. More stomach churning for Peggy.

The policemen were turning against the children now. Just as the chief constable wanted to confine Dorothy in a convent and Freddie in a religious reformatory, so the detectives longed to build a case that the little ones would have no chance of answering.

Her shoulders knocked into plaster walls, painted green and yellow. Two more steps were in her way. She jumped them but collided with a second manikin. She clung to him, hoping he'd stop her falling. For a long, slow motion, moment, they twirled in a comic dance before the figure brought her down in a perfect tackle.

A chaplain, working with his office door open, looked up from his desk. "Goodness, are you alone?" There was a trace of disbelief in his voice. He could understand the picture of a lady trying to protect her modesty as she gathered herself to her feet, but the idea that a civilian could have made it to the chief's floor without an escort seemed a remarkable lapse.

"Truly remarkable," he repeated aloud as he came to the corridor.

"I've an appointment to see the chief constable."

"Yes, yes. And you're alright?"

"I'm sorry about the gentleman," Peggy said, looking down at the sorry figure.

"Oh, don't worry about him; he'll mend. The chief constable, you say? You're Mrs Pinch, aren't you?"

131

How easy it would have been to say no, so that the chaplain wouldn't have to conjure up embarrassing pictures of her.

"Yes, quite." He could have been reading her thoughts. "You had better follow me."

Peggy had an uneasy feeling that the words didn't mean the same to her as they meant to him.

The chief constable, with a heavily embroidered smoking jacket over his tweed waistcoat, was already approaching, hand outstretched, as the door opened. "Why, Mrs Pinch, you do appear to be in a state. Come in and sit down." Keeping her away from his desk of official papers, he guided her towards an arrangement of armchairs and occasional tables at the other end of the room.

"You'll take a beer with me, chaplain?" he asked as he poured one for himself at an elaborate walnut cabinet.

Peggy was troubled to see that the chaplain was already seated in one of the chairs. "No, no. He can't stay. He mustn't."

"Don't be upset, Mrs Pinch," said the chief. "May I call you, Peggy?"

She was nodding and tugging at a loose tail of hair.

"The chaplain naturally listens to our welfare cases. You can rely on his discretion and —" the two men shared a chummy smile, "— he is rather good at sorting things out."

"But not in this case. You don't understand. It can't possibly be like that."

The chaplain rose to his feet. "I think that Mrs Pinch should share her worries with you, chief constable, and if necessary I can be brought in at a later stage."

The chaplain retired, Peggy declined a sherry but suggested a pale ale, and the chief selected a cigar to go with his beer and settled on one side of a table while Peggy allowed herself to relax in an opposite armchair. She noticed a smoking cap, hanging on a coat stand, which matched his fancy jacket.

"Now then," he said. "What is this all about?"

"Chief constable, I want you to acquire a warrant to search the bishop's palace."

He took a few seconds longer to light his cigar, allowing the match to flare to its full glory before shaking it out. He reached forward to drop the spent stick in an ashtray. "You know who murdered Ann Bidding?" he asked.

"I won't accuse anyone until I can prove it."

He went 'hmm'. The woman was being cautious. He thought, she's unlikely to suggest a search of the old bish's bin unless it was important. Peggy Pinch, he knew, didn't ask for things that she didn't expect to get. "I see why you wanted our chaplain out of the way. We'll find the evidence in the bishop's palace?" he asked. "Who are the suspects, Mrs Pinch?"

He drew heavily on his cigar, then tried to press his chin to his neck as the smoke came out of this nostrils. Looking over his spectacles, he said, "Mrs Pinch, you don't play gin rummy with the chief constable of the county. You place all your cards on the table. So, who are the suspects?"

"The woman was murdered between seven minutes past one and five and twenty past. You will agree that I had good reason to be watching the clock. Pinch had promised that I would be inconvenienced for only fifteen minutes; he over ran by three."

"Figures are not his strong suit."

Peggy took a good measure of ale, letting it run round her mouth before swallowing it. Her running and shouting through the corridors had left her thirsty. Delicately, she held back a burp. "Ann Bidding came to the police house seeking a confidential conversation with either Pinch or yourself, about her brother's situation. She looked through our kitchen window and, realising that it was not an appropriate moment, decided to wait in the garden shed. You will remember that Pinch had bolted the door but not locked it. Freddie Becker saw her and followed almost immediately. He, too, looked through the kitchen window."

"You suspect him?"

"Gary Willowby was watching from his garden gate and will say that Freddie was the only one to cross the road between those times. Dorothy was at her bedroom window and will support his evidence." She drank again. "I'm sorry, chief. I am very thirsty."

"Do you smoke? I have some cigarettes in the cabinet."

Peggy hesitated. It was unusual for her to smoke in the company of a man, but was it bad manners? The chief smiled at her confusion. "Shall we forget, Peggy, what the women might say in the post office? You have some difficult things to say; I'm sure a Black Cat would help." He pulled himself from the comfy chair, collected her empty glass and stepped across to the cabinet.

"I don't usually have more than one," she said. Usually, she could make a lady's glass of pale last for half an hour.

As he offered her the open cigarette box, he asked, "Did the children see the murderer?"

"Probably, but they don't know which of the suspects committed the crime." Peggy wanted to drink straightaway from her second glass but left it standing on the table. "Dorothy has not told me who assaulted her in the woods, and I won't ask her."

"The vicar has told me that Freddie has already given you one account."

"Then, the vicar shouldn't have told you." She picked up the beer glass. "Freddie wasn't the last one to visit our garden. I believe that our vicar also came calling. I'm sure he looked through the kitchen window."

"Quite a parade."

Peggy lit a cigarette and leaned back in the chair. She made a bit of a show, blowing out the first of the smoke. She was feeling light-headed now and needed to be careful not to say too much. "Yes. It does seem that half the village saw my husband chastising me. Perhaps, next time, he will give us all notice so that we can sell tickets. I'm sure the Church Restoration Fund would benefit." Oh Lord, was she really making light of it?

"You want me to have a word with him?"

"To sell tickets?"

The chief smiled. He tapped the cigar tip on his teeth. "No, to advise him that it is no longer lawful for a man to …"

"Please, don't speak of the matter in anything less than formal terms."

"…chastise his wife, reasonably or otherwise."

"Chief constable, my husband and I are not suited. You will

know that our marriage was arranged between Pinch and my mother. Her wish that I should make him proud of me was one of the last things she told me. I hope to deliver that wish one day." The chief was an easy man to talk to, she decided. Now, she approached the question that each of them had known was coming. "There was at least one other person who looked through the kitchen window."

"Yes. When I found that the vicar wasn't at home, I did return to the police house. I heard what was going on and, very briefly, looked through the window. This must be embarrassing for you."

"Very embarrassing. I will suffer the village gossip for years to come. Little children will be told stories about me, I'm sure."

The chief summarised. "You're telling me that the murderer followed Ann Bidding to the police house, saw that both Pinches were occupied and killed the poor woman in the middle of the commotion."

"I didn't take the inconvenience quietly, as you probably know."

"I'm afraid that I can confirm that the vicar was indeed party to the peep-show. I saw him retiring down your back garden path. He would have returned to the vicarage by the rough footpath at the back of the cottages."

"We call it the Waddie."

"If no one crossed the road ..." he considered.

"The murderer must have come from our side of the village. The vicarage, the Red Lion, the post office or the cottages."

"Yes, yes." He tapped the arms of his chair but getting up, yet again, seemed too much trouble. Instead, Peggy was treated to a bizarre game. The chief cleared his throat and make the loud 'ruff-ruff' bark of a setter. A police constable, carrying his helmet under his arm, entered without knocking and took the chief's order for a large sheet of paper, a pencil and rubber, a fresh cigar for himself and pale ale in a clean glass for Mrs Pinch. Peggy and the chief sat quietly while the constable served them efficiently.

When they were alone again, the chief hastily drew a map of the village, his fat and hairy fingers managing the pencil uneasily.

"The vicarage?" he asked, marking a significant square in the correct place and colouring it in.

135

"The household was full," Peggy explained. "The parlour and kitchen maids, the housekeeper and Mrs Fripps."

The chief moved on. "The Red Lion?"

"Our landlady and her cellar man."

"The post office?"

"Postmistress Mary was alone. Her brother was on the other side of the road, colluding with Janet McPherson. The other cottages were empty, apart from old Mrs Frayle."

"I see, so the postmistress has no alibi. And on the other side of the road, just so that I have the complete picture?"

"Ruby Becker and Dorothy were at home. Mr Becker was looking through the church accounts at the vicarage. Mrs Porter, Mrs Hornsby and Miss Carstairs were all at home."

The chief interrupted. "Dorothy's father was at the vicarage, you say?"

"Yes. He came home on the one o'clock bus and went straight to the vicarage. That was the arrangement. Chief, you must have seen Ernest Becker get off the bus."

"I can't say. When I returned from the vicarage, your Driver David was mooring the machine behind the war memorial."

Peggy asked. "And the vicar's wife?"

"In her garden, I think. Kneeling."

"She says she was," Peggy confirmed.

"I can't be sure." Then, after a moment's thought: "Yes, I'm certain she was kneeling. I think I looked at the back of her shoes. She said something. Now, what did she say? Ah, she was looking for Mrs Porter. That's what she said, 'Waiting for Porter.'"

Peggy unconsciously wrapped a curl of hair around the joint of her thumb. "Someone else has said that. Waiting for Porter."

As the chief pondered the facts, his yellow fingertips went to the whiskers that were growing up from his collar. It was like picking horsehair from an old sofa. "I see," he said again. "You haven't mentioned Verger Meggastones."

"He was at the top of the village, wandering to and from his cottage and the church."

"I see. The doctor, if I remember correctly, came running from your side of the road."

"But I've heard no suggestion that he spied on us."

"I see. I see, I see. Yes, yes."

"Chief, may I ask exactly what you saw when you walked to the vicarage and back?"

"Yes, yes," he repeated, still deep in thought. "I see. I see, I am quite an important witness at the crucial time. Well, I can corroborate most of what you have said. Young Willowby was at the garden gate. There, when I walked up the hill. And there, five or ten minutes later, when I came back. I saw the Dorothy girl at her window but I didn't see Freddie cross the road. That must have been while I was talking to the vicar's parlour maid. In fact, I have thought about this long and hard. Like your other witnesses, I am certain that I saw no one cross that lane in either direction."

"That eliminates Mr Becker," Peggy remarked.

"He has the strongest motive. His daughter had been raped, the day before."

"But not by Ann Bidding, and if he killed her, you would have seen him walking from the bus or the vicarage to the police house." Peggy trod carefully. "But you didn't see the vicar until you returned to our garden and spotted him hurrying down the back path."

The chief was surprised by the question.

"Otherwise, makes no sense," Peggy prompted. "You went to the vicarage to see the vicar. If you had seen him in the road, you wouldn't have continued to the vicarage. In either direction, you would have called on him to wait for you.

The chief looked thoughtfully at the burning tip of his cigar. "I didn't see him, Peggy. I simply didn't see him."

"And the parlour maid? Where did she say he was?"

"Your place."

"He was in the garden only long enough to see what was happening in our scullery, yet you didn't see him on the lane. Chief, it doesn't make sense."

It was obvious that Reverend Nigel had stayed at the kitchen window long enough to get a mighty good eyeful, but the chief saw no good in pointing out the reasoning. He said, "Peggy Pinch, you're ahead of me. For the life of me, I can't fathom who did it, but I'm content to play your game. Let the evidence emerge, and it will be the evidence, not you, that convinces me. I reckon that's good detecting. I am concerned about the verger and the post mistress. It seems to me that their alibis are especially weak."

"A number of us saw Mary come out of the post office," she reminded him.

"Let's work through this. At one o'clock, her brother arrives on the bus from town and is worried because the post office was closed. He has no key and he can't make the lady hear his knocking. He asks the verger to look for her. Why? Why ask the verger?"

When Peggy didn't answer, the chief suggested, "Because he knew she was likely to be in the vicarage annex and he knew that the verger would have access to that part. But he doesn't share his suspicions with the verger, not at that stage. However, Meggastones meets Freddie crossing the road, who mentions to him the annex is a good place to look. Why? Why would the lad know that?"

Peggy felt herself blush. "I don't know. Perhaps ... I can't really say."

"The vicar must have seen him, because he says Meggastones can give him an alibi. You see? He can't have seen one without seeing the other."

"We can check," Peggy said.

The chief was working slowly through the evidence. "By this time, I had finished my enquiries at the vicarage and met the verger at the gate. Now, I'm pretty sure that was no later than a quarter past one. So, let's say, that Freddie crossed the road shortly after ten past. Certainly, no earlier. I walked past the post office on my way to the police house but, damn it, I can't say whether the shed was open or not. And why did Brother Michael go to the schoolmistress? Did he think his sister was with her? Why? The earliest we know, for sure, that your friend Mary was at home was when she came running out to the road as the alarm was raised. A quarter to two. You see my point, Mrs Pinch. The postmistress might have been indoors all the time and the verger might have been busy at the vicarage during those thirty five minutes, but we must doubt both possibilities. Neither the man nor the woman can adequately explain their whereabouts throughout the time of your inconvenience, the time of the murder."

He was asking too many questions for Peggy to tackle. She was half way down her third glass of ale and she was ashamed to count three of her cigarette stubs in the ashtray. She was conscious that her talk of what had happened in her kitchen may have been unguarded; she tried to remember what, exactly, she had said, but it wouldn't come to her.

"I don't understand why I should search Bishop Harry's residence," the chief was saying. "It would be quite an unusual warrant, you understand. I cannot think of any precedence."

Peggy spoke softly, her head down, her fingers nervous. "You will find the book of Herbert's Extracts, stolen from the police house, Bredon's parish history taken from the school, two valuable books of butterflies and birds' eggs from the vicarage, and the missing book from the solicitor's office. I can give you the dates of three other thefts but I would not be able to identify the books. These were stolen either by the bishop himself or by Mr Bidding on his behalf. When he employed Bidding, a fee was paid into the funds of the Church Kneelers Embroidering Circle and passed to Bidding a few days later."

"Good Lord, Peggy, you're determined on scandal, my girl. A thieving bishop, my God. And this will lead us directly to the murderer?"

Peggy was ready to concede some uncertainty when she was interrupted by a half-hearted rumble, echoing from the far side of the building. At first, only the bubbles in their drinks seemed to shiver but then the windows rattled and an ashtray slid from the chief's blotter to the edge of his desk.

"That didn't sound like waterworks to me," he remarked.

There was shouting on the courtyard outside and boots were running along the corridors. Without warning, he emitted the setter's bark and the junior officer marched promptly into the room, his fingertips playing anxiously with the chin strap of the helmet under his arm. "Hawks, sir. Bi-cycle shed, sir. Sir, he seems to have blown it up."

139

"Nonsense. Wait for more news." The chief dismissed him and turned to Peggy. "I think a bomb would have brought us to our feet, don't you? Now, you were about to tell me what good it would do, searching the bishop's place."

The telephone rang. The chief hauled himself from his chair, trod idly across the carpet and addressed the instrument. "Can't possibly be true," he yawned. "What would the public think of their police force if they heard that people were trying to blow us up? Use your head, man. Come up with some story about people experimenting with new ways of solving crime. That's right, someone was experimenting and it went wrong. Of course, you must release him. No one will believe a word he says if he's still walking the streets. Now have two cars brought to the front doors and put Superintendent Evans in one. Mrs Pinch and I shall ride in the back of the other."

He held the telephone away from his ear while he made sense of the sound of shattered glass, coming up from the courtyard.

"Ah, that's better. Yes, arrest him for breaking a window. That's very acceptable, and make sure he's been drinking. The smell of wine on his breath. Yes, wine."

He returned to Peggy and asked if she'd like another drink while they waited. "The magistrates always like a mention of wine. It signifies lack of character in the accused."

CHAPTER TWELVE
Peggy's Butterflies

Two black police cars kept to the centre of the road as they progressed unhurriedly through the county lanes. In the lead, Superintendent Edmund Evans – fifty three years old and twenty two years in the force - sat in the front passenger seat with his hands deep in his raincoat pockets, his collar turned up and a gruff look on his face. It was a quarter past five so he had no chance of being off duty in time for his dinner appointment at the Kershaws. 'Should have taken father's advice and gone for the law,' he thought.

"Take it steady, constable," he said as they gathered speed downhill. There was always a risk of strays on these roads, not to mention free ponies.

When this folly was over, he would insist that something was done about Pinch's wife. He could put up with stories of her village pranks – slipping mice down the backs of other women, pouring goo over a rival's head and shouting matches in the street. He didn't care that she was the butt of jokes in every tearoom and on every refs bench in the county, but he would not have her roaming free through the passageways of headquarters, barging into the chief constable's private office and convincing him - and this Evans couldn't believe – convincing him to search a bishop's holy palace.

The driver slowed as they approached a minor crossroads. Evans sucked through his teeth; to cap it all, the man wasn't sure of his way. The evening was already dark out there, cold inside and the windscreen was misted

"To our left, do you think, sir?"

The car behind flashed its lights and pulled over to the right. Evans wondered if the chief constable wanted to get out and talk.

"Straight on, constable. The military are too touchy about policemen driving across their land. Don't upset the soldiers."

The driver pumped the pedal until he was able to engage gear, and the car jolted forward. The following car steered obediently into line and it seemed that, for the moment at least, the little detachment could press on with things.

"It's to do with the murder, sir, is that it?"

"Bishops don't do murder, constable," he said, then muttered aside, "although county superintendents might sometimes ponder on it."

Peggy and the chief constable shared the back seat in the second car. She was light-headed, her mind flitting from one thought to another, but it was the bumping and jolting of the car that made her regret drinking so much. She wished that the chief would talk and take her mind of it.

He looked straight ahead. He couldn't understand why he needed a driver and a bag carrier. Why was it when you gave policemen titles –drivers, posties, warrant officers – they felt excused from all other duties?

"A torch," he said.

A torch in a gloved hand reached over the back of the front seat. The chief switched it on and asked Peggy to hold it while he took a fragment of old card from his inside pocket. She shone the light on the unfolding page. It was a poison pen letter made up of words cut from a magazine and gummed to the back of a crude price list from Ruby Becker's shop.

"That tartar Mrs Pinch," he read. "An interesting word, don't you think? That was the first word to catch my attention. Tartar. I recognised it, you see. They used the term in this month's wireless handbook. Just as out of place there, as here."

The chief was allowing the paper to drift in and out of the torch beam so Peggy couldn't get a good look at it but had to piece the message together as she caught the separate words.

"I've checked," he said. "All the words have been cut from the same issue. Do you know anyone who takes it?"

"Half the gentlemen in our village, and Mrs Frayle. She's always bringing us up to date with wireless affairs."

He rested the card on his knee, holding it there with the cutting edge of his hand so that Peggy still could not read it. "That's good. Yes, I've never assumed it was put together by a man. In fact, quite the contrary. Yes, a very interesting word, tartar. It's a woman's word. It's what mothers call little boys."

"What it's all about, sir?"

"I've never heard a man say tartar."

Peggy said, "Mrs Porter." She had heard the woman use the word just yesterday.

"Mr Porter, you say? Yes, she's the type to send a poison pen. What do you think?" He looked again at the letter. "She says I'm to ask where that tartar Mrs Pinch was at the moment of the murder."

"You know the answer to that."

"But you weren't in the house all the time. Pinch shouted for you but couldn't make you hear."

Butterflies woke in her stomach, no more than a twinge but enough to add a flutter to her voice. "I was upstairs or at the front of the house."

"What did we say about slugs?" he asked. "You must have heard Pinch's solution to slugs. We discussed it for some time."

Peggy felt the colour come to her face as she searched for an answer. She was confused about the times. She wanted to say that she had come downstairs immediately the chief left the garden, but she knew that wouldn't answer his question. She didn't want to embarrass Pinch. She didn't want to prompt more gossip about herself. And she needed to relieve herself of the discomfort from drinking too much.

"Chief constable, why are you questioning me when you don't suspect me of murder?"

"Let's say that Ann Bidding wasn't murdered while you and Pinch were in your kitchen, but several minutes earlier. Let's say, you saw that I was keeping Pinch busy in the garden and used the opportunity to pop out when you wouldn't be noticed. If that is the case, Mrs Pinch, this letter may be very important indeed. It tells us that Mrs Porter – or whoever wrote the letter – knows the real time of the murder and was close at hand when it was done. Close enough to see you leave the house. I'm not saying that she killed the poor woman (I can see no motive for that) but she does become an essential witness."

Peggy looked out of the window at the passing hedgerows. "Are we nearly there?" she asked.

"Sergeant?"

"Another fifteen minutes, sir."

"Then I wonder if you would pull the cars over so that I might excuse myself."

There was a fidgety silence as the men took in her bizarre request. The driver thought that she was hoping to run off while his observer in the front seat judged that she was merely 'playing up'.

The chief said, "Sergeant, please indicate to the driver in front."

"Aye aye, sir."

It wasn't a straightforward communication. He steered to the left and travelled close to the verge for fifty yards. Then he speeded up before braking hard. Finally, he dowsed his lights for a few moments.

The lead driver sensed that there was a problem of some sort, relayed the information to his superintendent, then obeyed instructions to park in the middle of the carriageway. The second car drew up behind.

"Thank you, gentlemen," Peggy said primly. She drew back the door handle. "I shan't delay you longer than I have to." She left the car, crossed the road and picked her way carefully over a shallow ditch and into the blackness of the woodland.

The patrol cars stayed in line, their engines turning in the night, their motor-lamps burning poisonous yellow. Soon, the engines were overheating and both drivers weighed the possibility of boiling over against the aggravation of stopping and restarting a disgruntled engine. The lead driver thought that he heard her returning from the bushes but it was a young deer that landed recklessly in the middle of the carriageway. It hopped on her hind legs, turning in the air, then propelling herself back to the undergrowth. Already, Mrs Pinch had taken longer than it took to spend a penny. Four of the five men grumbled, each in their own way. Only the chief was content for Peggy to take her time. He wanted her to reconcile herself to parting with a secret.

"It's never straightforward with a woman in the car," remarked the officer in the front passenger seat. The lead car edged impatiently forward.

As if to emphasise that he was content to wait, the chief brought a cigar from his smoking waistcoat and made a great show of lighting it. The saloon soon filled with the rich smoke. The lead driver left his vehicle and, mindful not to follow the policeman's wife, used the ditch on the nearside of the road. The chief decided that the officer's manners had been prejudiced by the comfort of too much car driving and he would be returned to common beat duties at the earliest opportunity. When Peggy returned before the absent driver, the chief leaned forward to tap his man's shoulder. "Overtake," he instructed, "and don't wait for them."

Peggy settled herself in the seat. "This afternoon, Mrs Porter stopped me in your market place and accused me of having an affair with another man. That is untrue and unfair. But since that accusation I have been mulling over any -" Oh, Lord, what word could she use? "-doings that might have caused others to titter. Like you, chief constable, I do not believe that gossip is conjured from thin air. Generally there are grounds for suspicion."

The chief constable puffed. "Indeed."

"I've been worried about Dorothy Becker for some time, for weeks before Ethel Conlin's funeral. She is such a sad girl and I'm -" again, she searched for the right word – "I'm desperate that she should enjoy her youth in ways that I didn't. I have taken to talking to Mrs Willowby about this ..."

"Willowby? You mean, Becker?"

"Willowby, I mean, and such conversations are best shared away from eyes and ears so we meet, quite often in the nooks and hideaways around our little village. It was during one of these talks that she mentioned the teddy bear."

Ah, now we're getting somewhere, thought the chief constable.

"During my childhood, this teddy bear had been displayed on

the post office shelf and I was very jealous when it was bought for another girl. Eventually, it came into the hands of Dorothy Becker. Some months ago, I saw it lying in their front garden and I was tempted to pick it up. Ruby thought I intended to steal it. That is untrue, chief constable, but perhaps not unfair."

Signposts and military markings indicated that they were now trespassing on army land. The chief constable, increasingly discontented with his motor patrol officers, began to experiment with thoughts of reorganisation and regulation. "Yes, yes, Mrs Pinch," he said.

"Nothing goes unnoticed in our village, though I heard no more about it for three years. It seems that Mrs Willowby - rather a meek figure, you'd think – witnessed the incident and made up her mind to get hold of the teddy."

"Hmm," he grunted, giving attention to his cigar once more. "A teddy?"

"She promised that I should have this teddy bear but she expected something in return."

"Who promised?" He hadn't been paying proper attention. "Mrs Becker or …"

"Mrs Willowby. She had acquired the bear."

He puffed. "Yes, the teddy bear."

"She wanted to spend an afternoon together in the annex to the vicarage. I saw nothing wrong in that but the request – the bargain, if you like – seemed a strange one. I haven't given her an answer. Then on the day we buried Ethel, Mrs Willowby added something extra to her side of the transaction."

"Yes?"

"Somehow, she has also acquired an onyx ring that my late father used to wear on his little finger."

"Quite the magpie, your Mrs Willowby. And you think there is more to this?"

"She would like to make a present of it, when we are alone in the annex."

"You say, the day you buried Ethel. Have you discussed the liaison since?"

146

"Chief constable, it is not an assignation and I'll thank you not to make it sound like one."

"I'm sorry, Mrs Pinch. Please continue."

"When you were in the garden with Pinch, I noticed her waiting in the hedge behind our war memorial. I knew that she was waiting for me. Hoping for me, rather. So, yes, I did take that opportunity to pop out."

"No, no," the chief said, troubled. "This doesn't make sense."

"She was upset about Dorothy, upset about different things. During those few minutes together, she held my hand. Held my hand with a comfort that any spies might have found puzzling."

"The time, Mrs Pinch?"

"About twenty minutes to one. I was back home before one o'clock."

CHAPTER THIRTEEN
The Bishop's Gallows

The Gallows' Retreat stood at the crossroads of a pilgrims' way and an old smuggling route from the coast. Although it had not reopened as a travellers' rest since the armistice, the building kept much of its old character with broad downstairs windows for looking in rather than looking out, a large porch where passers-by could shelter from the rain without spending on food and drink, and two well-kept water troughs for thirsty horses. Lopsided stairs against an outside wall led to a thatched loft. The bishop had ordered the swinging sign to be taken down only two years ago and, over the oak front door, the quotation from Moliere, in quaint French, had been replaced by a verse from the apostles. He retained the hatch where wayfarers could knock for beer and cheese at eleven o'clock each morning, although the bishop's favourite joke was that few passers-by were as poor as the fledgling curates who came for counselling. (Wry humour, thought his diocese; they could not picture a lowly curate taking up his Lordship's time.) Still, Bishop Harry insisted that alms would be always available at this retreat even if the place was too out of the way to be called upon regularly. The house had its own public. More poachers gave than paupers received and the Gallows' regular vagrant insisted that he accepted no charity from the church. He paid for his suppers by keeping the household up to date with the goings-on in the woodland. Similarly, the old woman who lived in a hotchpotch of a shack in a nearby thicket fended for herself; she came to the hatch for nothing more than a chat with the bishop's cook. The tramp and the hag had a knack of timing their calls when the army doctor was spending an evening with the Lord Bishop. No one begrudged them a quick check-up.

Gallows was three miles from the nearest public road so the little convoy approached, quietly, headlamps dowsed and freewheeling whenever it could, along the military way that territorials had engineered to service their annual camp. Roake, the stable boy (Gallows had no horses but six well-furnished stables) saw them coming; he alerted the bishop's manservant and the cook, he called for his labrador and was ready at the redundant standard when the patrol left the concrete road and steered into the Gallows' clearing. He waved them to the rear of the building, his hands working with a precision that would have well satisfied the chief's controversial sergeant major for 'drill and musketry'. "Too clever by far," mumbled the superintendent. The boy had a history of petty troubles with the police and the bishop had taken him on to placate a well-meaning new hand on the local bench.

The disgruntled super told his driver, "As soon as we're in the house, you'll do a search. Never mind these stables. Go into the ditches and hedges that the lad can see from his bedroom. That's where you'll find things."

As the two motorcars circled and reversed in the tiny courtyard, the dog drew a broad circle, ready to discourage any breakaway. "Keep watch on the damned thing," moaned the superintendent. "If I get my way, we'll be taking Roake home with us. I don't want to start by running over his bloody sheep dog."

The dog's not a collie, thought the police driver but he didn't correct his superior. He knew that the superintendent bore a niggling ambition to gaol the lad, so this was no time to aggravate the man's temper. He'd already gone without his dinner.

Roake, wearing his working clothes and a rabbit skin cap with which the poacher had mockingly blessed him on his last birthday, was plain faced and courteous. Perhaps he didn't suspect the superintendent's prejudice. Either that, or he was insolently confident that he had the upper hand.

"This can't be the bishop's palace?" asked Peggy Pinch as the vehicles manoeuvred to a standstill.

The chief constable stubbed his cigar in an empty tobacco tin. "It's not. It's his gallows."

Peggy resolved to keep quiet until she was asked to speak. She watched, bemused, as a sequence of eccentric characters appeared on the stage. Each behaved as if they were in charge and each would have been well cast in a pantomime. First, the manservant in gaiters and a frock coat. He stayed on the back door step with his knuckled fingers interlocked over the fly of his trousers. "He wants to pretend that he's the landlord," said the chief, as he held Peggy's door open. "Do you think he's a poet? I'd bet a pint to a nickel that he is."

Next, the cook came striding from the front of the building. She was a fat woman with a bouncing bosom, a white cap and a full white apron without a splash on it, and a rolling pin which she carried like a club. She headed for the superintendent. "Now, don't you go picking on him," she demanded. "He's not been out of my sight for three days and, whatever you want him for, it doesn't take five of you."

"Bring them in here, Betty," the manservant called. "Leave Roake to wash the motors."

The lad had already collected two buckets of water and, without invitation, began to sluice them over the police cars.

"I would like to speak with the bishop," explained the chief.

"Then I want the rest of you, sitting in the cars." She turned to the chief. "The bishop won't wake up before his supper at eight. He likes to sleep after his afternoon tea. He's here for peace and quiet, you know that."

"Bring them indoors," the manservant said again.

The chief took Peggy to the back door where he repeated the purpose of his visit.

"What is it about?" asked this bishop's guardian, his hands still rudely at his crotch and his eyes narrowing as he studied the details of Peggy's face. The chief diverted this attention by tapping his knuckles on the doorframe.

"A very private matter."

The servant inhaled deeply, drawing in his nostrils and fluttering his eyelids. "Then I'll put you in the paupers' snug," he decided.

"There's not much light in there. Just you and the lady. The rest stay in the car like my Betty says."

His heavy heeled shoes knocked loudly on the old wooden floors as he took them through a succession of corners and up and down steps. They passed prints of fishes and woodland creatures on the leaning walls, and ducked beneath biblical quotations burned into the polished beams. The manservant didn't stand straight until he delivered them to the little room in a forgotten corner of the old inn.

"His eminence would like to offer you beakers of ale while you wait. He won't be down for another half an hour."

"Nonsense," growled the chief. "Wake the old chap up and tell him the police are here."

The servant bowed his head slightly. "Not for another half hour," he insisted. "His lordship sleeps until supper time. It is regular."

"Well, we're not regular my man. In fact, we are most irregular. Knock him up, I've said."

The man chose not to reply. He gave another slightest dip of his head and backed out of the room.

"Make yourself at home, Peggy, and don't be put off by all the nonsense."

For the next forty minutes, Peggy sat in an armchair with a fitted cover. A fringe hid the legs and the floral pattern was so faded that it was almost no decoration at all. Once or twice, she caught herself picking at the stitching of the beaded folds. The household kept a small fire burning in the grate, to dry the place rather than warm it, and the only lighting came from small oil lamps in each corner. The lamps were trimmed down low. The window was closed off with a pair of wooden shutters. The chief stood on the hearthrug in the familiar pose of a beat bobby with his feet apart and his hands behind his back, ready to cough politely and raise himself on the balls of his feet when any pause in the conversation suggested that the gesture was justified.

"It will take him twenty minutes to dress," Peggy conceded.

"The man's no more asleep than I am."

Outside, the superintendent was calling for the driver who had disappeared into the woods. The voice grew more impatient with each time that he repeated the officer's name. Peggy and the chief heard the manservant and cook whispering beyond the closed door of the snug but they couldn't make out what was being said.

"Chief, I'm not sure how to speak to a bishop."

He smiled but, before he could answer, the door creaked and another peculiar figure stepped into the room. The bishop wore a dressing gown, white cotton stockings, slippers with brass buckles and a sleeping hat with a bobble on a long tail that Dickens' cartoonist would have had much fun with. The chief caught Peggy's eye and winked.

He stepped forward from the rug and extended a hand. "My dear, Harry."

"My dear chief constable," responded the bishop, choosing not to use first names and making the pecking order clear. He didn't shake hands but acknowledged the chief's gesture with a nod of the head. "I've not dressed properly," he said. "My man indicated that it was urgent. If the matter's important enough to wake me, it's important enough not to dress for." He backed into a plush leather chair in the far corner, so that Peggy had to twist her neck if she wanted to face him and the chief couldn't sit in the third chair without losing sight of the bishop.

"You have a cigar, chief constable? You are rather famous for them."

Peggy remembered a similar request, possibly word for word, when he had intruded into the police house on one of his visits to the parish. The policeman obliged and proceedings were held up while the two men went through the business of lighting up. The manservant arrived with two half pints of beer on a tray, and a gill sized cup for Peggy. Really I've had enough, she wanted to say, but she had already decided not to speak.

"Now what's this about?" the bishop dreamed. Whatever it was, it was a waste of his time.

"You have stolen some valuable books. Others, you haven't stolen but engaged a thief to procure them for your benefit. Here are the details."

The chief's approach took both his listeners by surprise. Instead of asking questions or bothering with 'possibly' and 'maybe', he set out a detailed and unambiguous accusation. As he delivered his speech, in steadfast tones, Peggy understood all the difficulties that the local watch committee had experienced when engaging with him. Some might think he was a loose cannon, others might say he was trigger happy but both those tendencies could be managed. No, the chief was difficult because when the chief was right, he saw no point in diluting his case with compromise.

"You stole Herbert's Extracts from the police house, Bredon's parish history from the village school, two volumes of butterflies and birds' eggs from the vicarage, and the missing treatise from the solicitor's office. In three other cases, you employed Mr Bidding to steal books. You paid the wages into the funds of the Church Kneelers Embroidering Circle with instructions that Miss Conlin must pass those amounts to Bidding within the week."

"You can prove this?"

"Dates and signatures in journals will verify the sequence. Of course, the absolute proof will emerge when I ask the superintendent to search your palace library. One signal from me and he will be there faster than you can cover up the crimes."

"The crimes? Goodness me, Mrs Pinch, you have been busy." He itched his leg and, as Peggy twisted her head, she was alarmed to see, for no more than an instant, that the bishop's white cotton stockings were held in place by a woman's girdle. "I must dispute the ownership of the natural history testimonies from the vicarage. Surely, they are the property of the church and mine for disposal."

Peggy didn't look at him. She stared into the burning grate. "They were bequeathed to the village with the churchwardens responsible for their care. They were held in the vicarage, only because that was the best place for them." But the words meant nothing to her; she was asking herself other questions as her mind sifted through the truth of Ann Bidding's murder. Smoke, caught in a down draught, billowed from the chimney breast, its blue fingers curling as they rose to the timber mantelpiece. As it cleared, Peggy read the words made up of letters carved in little wooden blocks and glued to the trim. "The witnesses shall be the first to his death." The verse was so truncated that its true meaning was lost. But then, this verse had been badly used throughout this case.

"Oh, you both think you are clever," the bishop crowed. "But you don't begin to understand. The books that I have brought into safekeeping are far more valuable than their simple caretakers could possibly have known. Why, Bredon is worth more than eighty pounds. I have ensured that these treasures won't be lost. Don't you understand, I have built the palace library to be one of the most worthy of all collections? What do you propose? That it should now be scattered, willy-nilly. I will not return them."

"Restoring them to their owners will be a prerequisite of any arrangement," the chief insisted.

"So there need not be charges?"

"I'm afraid Lakey won't have it any other way. Yes, you will be charged."

"Where were you when Ann was killed?" Peggy asked, staring into the flames.

He spoke directly to the chief constable, his chin wobbling with anger, his slippered feet unable to keep still. "Do you think that my peers will convict me? Good Lord, man, we can't have a bishop of the realm brought to the House for a trial of thievery. Consider the implications of that. Think of the damage it will do. To the country, man. Think of the damage to our country. We've strikes, secret letters from communists and talk of mutiny in the navy. You want the common people to lose faith in their church at times like these?" He sat back in the high chair and wrestled for a solution. "Bidding will take the blame for all the offences," he declared. "He won't let me down but I insist on being fair with the man. I will put the word out that he is to serve no prison sentence."

"Where were you when Ann was killed?" Peggy asked again, still not lifting her face from the flames.

"Great Scott, woman! You think I killed her?"

For two days, she had been so sure of the murderer's identity. Thank God, she had not given voice to that conclusion because, now, she saw the truth emerging from the little fire in this tiny corner of the Bishop's Gallows Retreat.

She said, pressing the last piece of the puzzle into place, "No, but were you in the village when she was slaughtered?"

The chief was ready with his professional skill. "Mrs Pinch, if the bishop agrees to answer your question, need it go further than this room?"

"Sir, he has no need to answer. But if the bishop was not in the village, please let him deny it and tell me I'm wrong."

The flames had reached an awkward knot of log. It spat and spluttered, then spurted petulantly.

"I was last near your village on the day of the funeral but no closer than the woods. Whatever else has been said, whatever, is no more than country folks' fancy for witnessing fairy tales and ghosts."

"A car," she said. "I need to return to the police house before I'm too late."

The bishop's supper was announced. The chief constable requisitioned use of a telephone and, for a ludicrous ten minutes, Peggy Pinch witnessed her rescue plan in jeopardy. The force had only five vehicles, Sergeant Robbo explained. One was broken, the chief constable already had two, a fourth was too far away and the fifth had no driver on duty. "Then send a motorcyclist to St Faith's. He's to carry Pinch back to his police house but neither officers are to enter until Mrs Pinch arrives. Sergeant, this is urgent business." He replaced the receiver and faced Peggy. "The superintendent will take charge our evidence in the bishop's palace. I shall stay here and agree terms with the old fool while my driver takes you home. I've too much respect for you, Peg, to ask what's in your head but I sense you are ready to stand in the way of danger. I don't doubt your courage but I forbid you to enter that house without my officer at your side."

Five minutes later, when he politely settled her into the back seat of the car, she said, "Don't you see? We've been asking who crossed the road when, all the time, we needed to identify who didn't."

His whiskered throat was itching as he watched the car disappear into the shadows of the woodland. "Who didn't? But the whole lot of them didn't."

CHAPTER FOURTEEN
They Call It Bloody Cottage

The policeman talked all the way. He and Pinch had been young constables together before the war. Lord, he laughed, they had been a couple of scallywags. He could tell Mrs Pinch a thing or two about her husband. But Peggy didn't listen to the stories. They were just a stream of words that filled the time between the Gallows' Retreat and her village.

"We'll be neighbours before long. The chief has promised me Brevitt's beat when he retires. It'll see me out nicely. Mind, I won't let the old man down. I've ideas for the place. I'm sure he'll let me stay on for a few years. What do you think of that, then? You and old Cyril neighbours? Pinch always called me Dangerous Cyril because I'm not." The police car creaked on its beams as he decelerated through a corner, the front bumper collecting stalks and leaves from the bank on the exit. "The chief said I'm to hurry but I've never liked driving fast. A chap can't hurry on these country ways."

Peggy tensed herself and pushed back on her seat. "The crest might surprise you," she warned. "The road narrows and ..."

"Oops, my golly!" he exclaimed and jiggled the wheel. At last, they were heading for home.

"I'm looking forward to spending the last years of my service with Pinch close at hand. Like a full circle, don't you think? There at the beginning and there, together again, at the end. I think I shall buy a dog. That will do, don't you think? Yes, I'll buy a dog as soon as I get the keys to Brevitt's beat cottage."

156

"Please drop me at the church," she asked. "I will walk down the lane to the police house."

He slowed to a stop at the kissing gate. "I can't do that, Miss Peg. The chief said I wasn't to leave you alone. No matter what you said, he said." He turned off the engine and worked and reworked the switch until the car lights died.

"Constable Cyril, I have walked up and down our village street four times a day for twenty-five years. I'll come to no harm. I'm going to sit on the memorial bench and wait for something to happen. You will be able to watch me from Pinch's bedroom window."

"You know who it is then? You know who butchered the woman?"

"We'll both know for sure within half an hour," she said.

"I don't know what to do and that's a fact. I don't mind going against the chief but I've a responsibility to old Arthur. Me and him being chums once upon a time."

Peggy was already climbing out of the car. "Then keep careful watch from the window, Cyril. Don't use your lights on the way down and park out of sight."

He was still talking up his prospect of a village beat as Peggy closed the door. "Everyone will look forward to it," she said kindly and stepped away as the car drifted forward.

She stood in the shadow of the verger's hedge and watched the policemen roll his motor silently down the hill. He steered left before the ford and the car disappeared behind the school. She smiled as she thought of Pinch's nickname for his old friend. 'Dangerous.' Peggy decided that it would be difficult to find a less dangerous policeman.

A lamp burned at Miss Carstairs' window, someone was working in the dark behind the Red Lion and the church door was ajar. Curtains hung straight at the windows of Plumtree Cottage and no little faces peered out. Peggy's footsteps seemed to echo against every wall as she walked down from the green. She altered her pace and strained her ears for any sound that she was being followed. Her neck was cold and she ruffled her coat collar. At the memorial bench, she sat down and waited in the dark.

She knew that the murderer was in the hedges behind her but she didn't turn around. She heard Mrs Frayle open the side door of her cottage and deposit a package on the step for collection in the morning; the old lady's bedtime drink and clay hot water bottle were ready.

Verger Meggastones, completing his perambulation, emerged from the night-time grey. He had an extra scarf round his neck and a hessian sack over one shoulder. He carried his walking stick to poke things with.

"I'm pleased to see you're out of the cell, verger," Peggy whispered when he was two steps from her.

"Loosed from the drunk tank, they say in penny dreadfuls." He sat down, stretched out his legs and rewrapped the scarf. "Little Freddie set me free. I caught his attention while he was doing a piddle in your back garden. He knows how to unlock your back door, the little bogger. He took the cell key from its hook and unscrewed in time for lunch in the Lion." He sniffed the night air. "He had half a thought of blackmailing me but I soon set him straight on that point. I think – don't you – that honour is satisfied on both sides?"

"It's better that Pinch knows nothing about it," she agreed naughtily, saying nothing of Pinch's promise to bloody the verger's nose. "You've no mind to say sorry?"

"Have you?"

"Verger Meggastones, I have nothing to apologise for. Well you know that."

"Well, I can't say I'm sorry for taking a fancy to you. But as for the time and place, yes, I'll say sorry for that." He drew himself to his feet, stepped across to the waste box on the noticeboard and, clump by clump, filled his sack with the village litter.

"It's not your week to keep it clear," Peggy remarked.

"Half an hour ago it occurred to me that Janet McPherson's not here to take her turn so I've stepped in, uninvited." He shook the sack. "This lot will burn down well on my bonfire."

"I was hoping," she said, "that no one would clear it, but perhaps it won't matter."

The verger waited for Peggy to explain further. When she didn't, he dipped his head. "I'll say goodnight. Don't be out long, Mrs Pinch." Leaning on his stick more than he needed, he swung the sack over his shoulder and trod his way homewards.

A few minutes later, Ernest Becker came to his front gate. He had seen a figure on the bench and wanted to be sure who it was. He seemed to hesitate, as if he wanted to speak with Peggy, before turning his back and walking silently to the side door of his cottage.

The village lane was empty now. There was no sign of the schoolma'am's cat or the post office collie. Peggy heard a motorcycle, far away, and guessed that Pinch and his colleague were climbing the hill from Thurrock's farm. Slowly the chief constable's directions were being played out. She had less than twenty minutes to prove the murder.

There was just a waft of lamplight from her own bedroom window; 'Dangerous' had taken up his post. At last, Queen O'Scots trod forward from a grass verge and hopped onto Miss Carstairs' gatepost. A feline sentry, if ever there was one.

"You can come out," Peggy said.

With hardly a sound, Baby Michael stepped out of the hedge. He looked tired and limp but his pale eyes were hard-set and determined.

"You wanted to make sure that the waste box was cleared, didn't you? But you're too late, Michael. Driver David has already retrieved the wireless magazine. I'm sure he'll still have it when the chief constable calls for it as evidence."

"They won't hang me for that," he said defiantly.

"But it was important to make the police think that the murder happened earlier than it did, wasn't it? That's why you sent the nasty letter." She got to her feet. "I've cold broth in my scullery. Let's you and I heat it up on the stove. No one's at home."

Peggy guided him to the middle of the road as they walked. "Dorothy hasn't spoken about what happened, Michael. I'm sure she never will, so you mustn't hurt her again."

"I don't care what you say. I don't care what you think. The police won't have enough to charge me."

No one watched. In seventeen minutes, the village would be up and dressed and wrapped in death, but Peggy and her neighbours knew none of that as she led Baby Michael towards her home.

"Little pieces join together to make one big piece," she said. "The poison pen letter is important and the fact that you were missing from Ethel's funeral when Dorothy was attacked. But the crucial question has always been who crossed the road. Or, rather, who didn't. The children were watching from one o'clock until a quarter to two and, through all that time, no one walked from one side of the road to the other. At five past, you were seen on this side so you couldn't have been with Janet McPherson, unless the vicar has lied to us and I don't think he has. You knew that people were pointing fingers at Janet so you convinced her that she needed an alibi. She didn't realise that it was she who was giving you an alibi."

"It's not enough."

The house had the chill of a home where no fire had been lit that day. Peggy stepped inside and listened for Michael's first footstep behind her. The kitchen tap dripped and the curtain moved in the draught as Michael closed the door behind them. Did he manage to make the latch click more slowly, more loudly than usual?

Damp from the walls hung heavy in the air, nowhere creaked and the mice stayed quiet.

She said nothing about the murder as she lit the stove and placed the pan of broth over the flame. Keeping her coat on – thank heaven for that instinct – she led him into the dark parlour.

"The mystery woman, Michael. You told Sergeant Fisher that you met her at the top of the village. Is that true, Michael? No one else saw her in the village that afternoon. A mystery woman whom no one's seen on that day or after."

"Well, I saw her! She was there!"

"And the poor woman who died? Did you see her cross the road? You told Fisher you did."

"I – Maybe I was confused. Maybe I mixed them up. I think, now, yes, it was the mystery woman all along."

Peggy pursed her lips. It would have been sensible to sit him in one of the armchairs and encourage him to talk. Instead, Peggy felt

160

her anger get the better of her. "What about this nonsense rhyme she told you?"

"It wasn't a nonsense rhyme. It was from the Bible."

She wanted to yell at him but, with her fists clenched in her coat pockets, kept her voice taut but moderate. "You thought she was telling you to leave no witnesses. That's why you killed Ann Bidding. Because she saw you rape poor Dorothy."

"Don't say that! It's a horrible word!"

She turned her back. "Michael, I've found your woman with awkward shoulders. That afternoon, she walked up from Thurrocks Farm. If you saw her, it was in the woods, just half a mile from where you left Dorothy."

"Who is she? Can you name her?"

No, Peggy had to concede. No, it was improbable that the bishop in a woman's clothes would ever be called to account.

"Then they'll not hang me for it," he repeated.

She spun round. "Oh, they will, Michael," she shouted. "When they learn what you did to little Dorothy and how savagely you killed Ann Bidding, they'll hang you good and proper."

He thrust a hand to his back and brought a butcher's knife from his belt. "You've never liked me!" he spat. "You've always ignored me. Do me for murder, will you? Go on, call me 'Baby' one more time."

"Don't be so silly!"

He went for her. Peggy felt the shoulder of her coat tear, she yelped but didn't realise that he had cut her until the blood started to stream down her sleeve.

Dangerous Cyril pushed his way through the staircase door. "I've heard enough!"

She saw Michael smile as he turned to the man and, giving himself no time to think, drove the knife deep into Cyril's abdomen.

Cyril's fat round face ballooned, turning crimson, then purple, then blue. His tongue swelled, forcing his mouth open in a horrible shape. His eyes reached forward from their sockets. Peggy watched his voice reach down to the pit of his belly, searching for a scream that no one would ever hear. He stepped back, his hands spread out

161

for support but there was none to find. The policeman toppled forward, turning in the last moments of his fall so that he landed on his back.

Peggy covered her face and screamed. "My God! You've killed him!"

Michael staggered forward until he was standing over the policeman's body. He was panting like an animal as he bent his neck and took in all that he had done. His black hair was wet with sweat and exhilaration. Turmoil burned on his face. His forearms and legs were filled with a livid strength he had never known before.

He threw his head back and howled, "Leave no witness to cast the first stone!"

The blood had turned him mad.

He brought his head round in a low arc until he was staring up at Peggy's face. "You've never been my friend," he scowled.

"My God, Michael! No!"

Her knees gave way as he grabbed her throat in his right hand and raised the dripping knife in his left high in the air.

Gunshot exploded in the little room, bringing timber splinters and plaster down with the dust that billowed from every corner. Through the settling mist, she saw Mr Becker standing steadfast with his shotgun, ready to fire again. Peggy gasped for breath but she could find no air in the acrid smoke. Her throat constricted. Her lungs squeezed, as if some giant hand was squashing a sponge inside her chest. She forced her eyes wide open but already they were losing their sense. A black cloud swam over her.

It felt as if she were out for only seconds but when she came to her tiny parlour was full of familiar voices. The doctor was there, Miss Carstairs and the vicar's wife. Pinch was barking orders and a stranger was shouting that the chief constable was on his way. Ruby Becker was wailing in another room. Mrs Porter was trying to stop people from emptying the cupboard of Peggy's best linen but no one answered her. Still, Peggy couldn't see. Someone was tying off a bandage to her shoulder; another was helping her into Pinch's favourite armchair. When, at last, the blackness slowly gave way to grey fuzzy shapes, she saw her best tablecloth draped along Cyril's length. A hand towel from her kitchen had been tossed over Baby Michael's dead face. She saw Mr Becker's long legs through the open kitchen door; he was seated at the breakfast table. Then old Mrs Frayle took Peggy's cold hand in hers and said that she was going with her to the vicarage. "The men have got some cleaning up to do."

At a quarter past two that morning, when the village was wide awake not because it couldn't settle but because there was so much to do, Porter, Carstairs and Moorcroft laid down the law in the post office parlour. Mary was not to speak of leaving. She was their postmistress and she belonged in the village. They promised that folk would gather round and Michael's part in this horrid affair would never be mentioned. There would be no wagging tongues. Wasn't there a nephew who might come and stay?

CHAPTER FIFTEEN

A Fete in May

Somehow, the village survived winter and spring. Michael was buried, with no stone, in a corner of the graveyard and Ruby Becker let it be known that neighbours should lay flowers as they saw fit. She was heard to say, more than once, "The Beckers have taken their price."

Janet McPherson – in the chair since Mary's prompt resignation – had proposed that the church kneelers competition should be cancelled for that year but St Faith's wouldn't hear of it. They submitted the sorry remnants of their best needlework with bewildered stories of fabrics that gave way like shoddy. No one could believe how it had happened. The judging panel announced its inevitable decision before Easter and everyone agreed that Dorothy should be invited to accept the plate, on behalf of the St Stephen's Church Kneelers Embroidering Circle, at the May fete.

Isabelle Fripps and Peggy were hesitant. They had spent many hours trying to put the young life together again and they insisted that the proposal shouldn't be put to the girl until she had the confidence to decide for herself. Easter came and went before Dorothy learned to manage even the mildest of the unexpected interruptions that punctuated her day. With three weeks to go, the policeman's wife and the vicar's wife agreed that their patient wouldn't be able to cope with such a public appearance. But Dorothy was ahead of them. Peggy called one morning to find her feeding the family of ducks which had made their home in the Beckers' garden. Dorothy announced that the Scots mistress wanted her to appear on the garden party platform. She was surprised that Peggy hadn't heard about it. She laid down three conditions; she wouldn't be expected to speak, she wouldn't need to be seen at the party before time, and would be hurried back home as soon as she accepted the presentation. Peggy reminded her that she had plenty of time to change her mind and knelt down to tender stale bread from her coat pocket.

The busting of Meggastones' nose was a tale that improved with each telling and, because he wore the patch and bandages for several weeks, the story had plenty of room to grow. Some people said that the outraged husband had constructed a complicated trap so that when the verger trod on a loose slab, a sequence of springs and ropes shot a shovel blade into his face. Others believed that the bobby had recruited the cellar man and the roofer. The three of them ambushed Meggastones one night and spun him around until he was too dizzy to know which of his assailants delivered the final blow. Young Freddie Becker liked this story so much that he composed a song to go with it. He was heard singing it one night as Poacher Baines fiddled on the churchyard wall. The truth was simpler. Pinch was waiting in the Red Lion's yard at one o'clock one morning and caught the verger with one smart blow, delivered in the dark. The two gentlemen didn't need to discuss the trouble and within a fortnight they were breakfasting, drinking and smoking together. The produce show at the vicarage garden party left no doubt that their horticultural rivalry was as vibrant as ever.

Joe Bidding wasn't prosecuted, the true story of the book thefts remained untold and the bishop avoided the village. There is no police record of the Christmas Eve burglary when a slight feminine character, dressed in black, broke into the bishop's palace. Three weeks later, Reverend Nigel, popping into the annex to see how the parish library was coming along, noticed the missing books on the top shelf. That afternoon, he pinned his own proclamation on the church notice board. The books were village property and would be kept under lock and key.

For Peggy, one other matter remained to be settled. She made a list of those men who had peeped at her bare sit-me-down on the murderous afternoon. Freddie was a child and Michael was dead, but she resolved to collect her exhibition dues from the other two characters.

The vicar was easily caught. She walked into the church on the afternoon of twelfth night and found him lodged in the rafters. "Trying to dislodge this blinking nest before they come back. Every Sunday I have to look at it from the pulpit and, excuse me Peggy, but I've had enough of it." At that moment, he lost his footing, grabbed a timber with one hand, wedged his other arm in the crook of a gable but was left with his feet dangling. Peggy promised that help was on the way. She brought a table from a back room, climbed on top but, instead of steadying him so that he could clamber down, she relieved the vicar of his shoes. "They will be in my garden, Reverend Nigel, just below the kitchen window. But remember, it would be very rude to peek inside." She returned the table to the vestry.

She was reluctant to tax the chief constable in a similar way. He had taken to visiting the police house once or twice a month and something of a friendship had grown between them. But she never doubted that, on the bloody afternoon in November, he had spied through the kitchen window with an indulgence akin to the greediness of a fat boy spying melting buttered hot muffins. Even so, she might have excused him but he began to call more frequently than good manners allowed and, whenever he watched her from behind, Peggy had a sixth sense that he was imagining, if not remembering, the shape of her rear end. One afternoon, he and Pinch were smoking in the parlour when she took the old man's fidgeting to be a signal that he would excuse himself to their outside lavatory before long. She replaced the roll of tissue with leaves of Freddie Becker's paintings which weren't quite dry. She made sure that she was alone in the kitchen when he returned. "I have always thought – haven't you? – that back windows are for those inside rather than passers-by."

"Umph," he groaned and shuffled uncomfortably through to the parlour.

When the sun shone on the vicarage garden party in May, the old wives said that the good weather showed that God had forgiven them, once again, for allowing wickedness in their midst.

Weeks before, Ernest Becker had put the word around that he wouldn't visit the fete. It would be quite wrong for him to be seen on such a merry day. The experience of shooting a man had delivered him to quiet moods and uneasy sleep. Then, unknown to others, Mary took him aside and insisted that he should take part in the celebrations. It was their way of showing how good the village was, she said. "It's about looking forward, don't you think? Neither of us want to listen to the past. If you're not there, Ernest Becker, it's not over. Remember the day when I was chosen to lead the embroiderers? Well, I overheard Peggy Pinch say to Miss Carstairs what a colourful clown you'd make. Ernest, I can't get the notion out of my head." And so, after the vicar's opening speech, Becker cycled into the games ring with huge slippers on his feet, a curly wig and a jacket that hooted whenever he clamped his elbows. Ten minutes later, he was booked for the Christmas party.

By three o'clock, the fete was in full swing. The vicar and the bobby walked around in duty dress and Mrs Porter was busy-bodying in a way that, for once, was helpful rather than intrusive. Young Gary invested his pocket money on a bundle of books in a wicker basket and Freddie rummaged through a crate of old tools, producing a redundant chisel handle which he was allowed to take away, free of charge. He knew that he could whittle it into a good shape of a mouse and spent the rest of the afternoon fingering it in his trouser pocket. Mrs Frayle judged that Mrs Willowby had made the best hat but she refused the prize because she was organising stalls that afternoon and it wouldn't have been proper. So first prize went to her daughter Grace who, if truth were told, was responsible for the needlework on both hats. "Quite remarkable," said Mrs Porter and lobbied for the young girl to be given an immediate place on the Church Kneelers Embroidering Circle.

Pinch, to much applause, won the modeller's award for his miniature of a loco from the Tay Bridge disaster.

This year, there was a wireless competition for the first time. The

Vicar presented his hand built and, he said, hand veneered set which he would give to the village library. It was probably the best on show but he decided not to submit it to the judges. Mr – husband of Mrs – Porter showed a carefully constructed replica of a modern ship's radio which he demonstrated throughout the afternoon and managed to elicit a response from a craft in the Thames estuary. However, the basket of fruit went to Driver David. His apparatus looked a ramshackle business but a great cheer went up when he received a signal, taken to be a foreign language in Morse.

The gardening competition was most keenly watched. Although everyone clapped as each class was decided, there was only one judgement that mattered. The competition between Pinch and Meggastones for the best vegetable. This was always going to be a contentious matter so the vicar had decided that the tobyman from the town market should be brought in as an independent judge. At a quarter to four, an eerie tension fell across the vicarage lawn. The cellar man and the roofer stood by to protect the adjudicator from any dispute. Everyone pushed forward from the rope that had been laid as a boundary. Pinch and Meggastones were surrounded by their respective camps. The judge wanted to declare a dead heat but no one would have that so the gavel went down for the verger. Wisely, Mr Meggastones didn't push himself forward and Pinch quelled the rising grumbles by agreeing with the decision. There was an ugly moment when someone hinted at foul practice but Pinch stamped on that too.

And so, at four o'clock, attention shifted to the stage, decorated with the Union Jack and bunting representing the wartime allies. This was Dorothy Becker's moment. Because she had refused any notion of wearing a party dress, her mother had been up all night altering the formal dress that she had worn for her own confirmation. Steady and determined, Dorothy climbed the three steps with the composure of a young woman. She delivered three lines, which she had composed herself, congratulating the runners-up and thanking everyone for their hard work. Everyone sensed that a loud cheer would have been out of place, so they clapped in a disciplined but enthusiastic manner.

At that moment, ten year old Gary Willowby decided that he would marry the girl. It wasn't love or infatuation, but a straightforward recognition that no one would be able to care for Freddie's sister as he meant to do, so it was his job to hold himself in readiness. He had much to do before he would be worthy of her, of course. He walked home with his hands in his pockets and his head bowed, duty being a hard taskmaster.

By eight o'clock, the villagers were in their homes. Miss Carstairs and Queen O'Scots were asleep at their hearth, Mrs Frayle was reading a library book on her porch and Poacher Baines was in his woodland hut, dressing some fresh fowl.

Peggy brought two suppers into her parlour. "A good day for young ones, don't you think?"

He was sitting in his favourite armchair and looking out over the street as he smoked. "Yes, the village is in good hands," he said. He turned to look at her. "You were putting her off, all afternoon. Mrs Willowby. She wanted to walk around with you."

At the top of the hill, Isabelle Fripps walked into her husband's study and said that it had been a good day for the Willowbys.

"Yes, they're coming out of themselves," he said. He looked up from his correspondence. "Who's with Mary?"

"There's a lamp at her bedroom window." She settled herself in her armchair and took up some neglected knitting. "You must be very pleased, the way people came together."

The village parson had been thinking along those lines. "All round, I think it was a good day for the Pinches."